$1.25

No sentry. No dogs. Nothing.

Barrabas frowned. He found it hard to believe that they had really caught Karl Heiss napping. But if they had, Barrabas was going to make damn sure he never woke up.

Cautiously, the white-haired man rounded the rear of the BMW in a crouch, picking up speed as he moved for the next vehicle, about twenty feet away. He had gone about four feet when his luck abruptly turned.

One second the way was clear, the next, he was staring across the BMW's trunk lid, face to face with a very startled sentry. The man was wearing external body armor, just like Barrabas, and he had an Uzi SMG in his hands.

The guy was startled, but definitely a pro. He recovered the same instant Barrabas did. They both brought their guns around. The sentry had a slight advantage because his weapon was shorter, pointed quicker.

Before Barrabas could get on track, he was tracked. The quick burst of autofire caught him full in the chest.

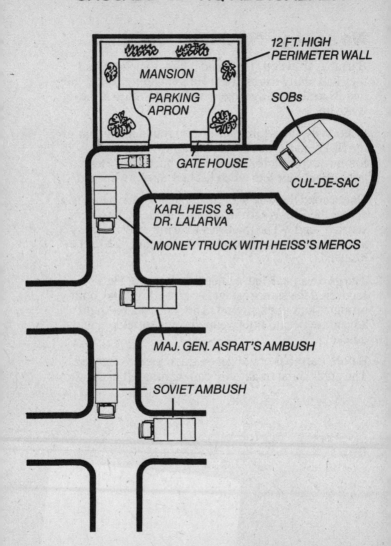

"CRUSADE '85" HQ ADDISABABA

12 FT. HIGH
PERIMETER WALL

MANSION

PARKING
APRON

SOBs

GATE HOUSE

CUL-DE-SAC

KARL HEISS &
DR. LALARVA

MONEY TRUCK WITH HEISS'S MERCS

MAJ. GEN. ASRAT'S AMBUSH

SOVIET AMBUSH

SOBs
VULTURES OF THE HORN

JACK HILD

A GOLD EAGLE BOOK FROM
W RLDWIDE

TORONTO • NEW YORK • LONDON • PARIS
AMSTERDAM • STOCKHOLM • HAMBURG
ATHENS • MILAN • TOKYO • SYDNEY

First edition January 1986

ISBN 0-373-61610-4

Special thanks and acknowledgment to
Alan Philipson for his contributions to this work.

Printed in Canada

1

Dawn breaking behind her, Esther Walatta climbed slowly down the hillside, bare brown feet picking the path of least discomfort through the slope's litter of sharp stones. Faint purple light tinted the broad, barren plain below. Here and there, pinpoints of orange glowed feebly: tiny, scattered, dung-fueled fires, smoldering in the morning chill, their raw, pungent smoke drifting up to her on the breeze.

She clutched the small rag bundle tighter to her chest. Aside from the frayed cotton shift she wore, it was all the property she had. Carefully wrapped against the night air in the tattered yard of muslin was her baby son, Deneke. The infant lay still in her arms, too weak from hunger to cry, too weak to try to suckle at her empty breasts. Esther walked faster, keeping her gaze on the steep and broken ground as she descended, afraid to stare too long at the refugee camp exposed by spreading daylight, afraid it would disappear. She walked as she had every night, all night, for the past month, the flow of soft, careful steps like the rhythm of her breathing or the beating of her heart.

Only when she neared one of the little fires did she look up from her feet. A fierce smile split her gaunt face, peeled back her lips and bared her teeth. The figures sitting slump-shouldered in the shallow depression in the dirt, backs braced against the low wall of heaped earth that served as a windscreen, did not return her greeting. Wreathed in cottony dung smoke, these creatures of no evident sex, with shaved heads, jutting ears, skin stretched drum-taut over cheek and chin, looked straight at her and saw no one.

It was understandable.

They did not know her. They did not know all she had lost or all she had accomplished. Triumphant smile undimmed, Esther Walatta moved on with her baby, past the cluster of living ghosts, toward the sprawling main encampment.

From a quarter of a mile away she could hear the fragile, erratic coughing of sick children and the shrill wailing of solitary mourners. She stepped cautiously into a sea of recumbent bodies, more people in one place than she had ever seen before. In rags they lay, a few in shallow furrows scratched into the hard dirt, fewer still in crude conical huts made of stacked sticks; but most of them, by the thousands, just curled up on the ground, under the open sky. It was like crossing a vast and terrible

battlefield. With the rising of the sun the pros-
trated multitude began to show signs of life and in
so doing, stirred clouds of fine, choking dust that
mingled with the overhanging pall of acrid smoke.

She stepped around and between them, heading
for a row of corrugated tin shelters in the center of
the camp. As she walked, the sun's warmth roused
vast swarms of flies. They landed on her mouth, her
nose, her eyes, everywhere at once. She brushed
them away with her free hand but they were back
immediately, seeking her body's moisture. Too
many to deal with, they had to be ignored.

Under a blackened metal awning great pots of
watery porridge bubbled over wood fires. Esther
spoke to one of the men stirring the pots.

"Give my baby some food," she said.

The man gestured with his free hand at a building behind her and said something she could not
understand.

"Food for my baby," she repeated insistently.
Her own hunger had long since vanished. The
burning cramps, the desperate gnawing had faded
after weeks of starvation, replaced by an overwhelming numbness as her body methodically set
about consuming itself.

Another cook interrupted. He spoke Tigre, the
language of her province. "Before you get food or
medicine you must see the doctor over there. Get a

paper chit from the doctor. Trade the paper for food. Those are the rules here.''

A line was already forming when she got there. Black women with babies queued up in front of an open doorway hacked from the sheet-tin wall. A white woman with very short black hair in a white coat was looking at each of the mothers and children and passing out little pieces of paper.

As she waited her turn, Esther held Deneke close and rocked him gently. Over the chaotic sounds of the awakening camp she began to sing very softly to him. She sang him a song of plenty, a song about fat red tomatoes and golden squash, great crisp cabbages and stacks of warm *injera* bread dripping with honey.

DR. LEONA HATTON pinched the skin on the baby girl's rib cage, then on the backs of her arms and thighs. The child did not stir at her touch; it didn't even have the strength to blink the flies from the corners of its milky, clouded eyes. Through the stethoscope its heartbeat was thin and fast. Too far gone. The white woman turned her attention to the child's mother. The woman was horribly emaciated, beyond whatever slim help the food distribution center could provide. Calories alone would not save either of them at this point. The doctor knew that both mother and daughter would be dead within twenty-four hours. That meant no chit. Food was in such pitifully short supply it could only be given to those with a 50-50 chance for survival.

Dr. Leona Hatton looked the woman straight in the eye and shook her head.

The mother held out her hand for the piece of paper she knew was not forthcoming, tears cutting dark tracks down the dusty hollows of her cheeks.

Leona Hatton clasped the woman's trembling hand tightly between her own and, her gaze still straight on, again shook her head. The pain in the back of the doctor's throat was a dull knife blade slowly twisting, but she remained dry-eyed. Lee Hatton did not weep with her dying patients at Barem camp. There were not enough tears to go around.

A large black hand lightly touched the refugee woman's skeletal shoulder. She turned to stare up at Claude Hayes, his powerfully muscled, ebony chest and arms already gleaming with sweat under the khaki athletic T-shirt. He bent down and spoke Amharic to her, in a deep, soothing voice. She stopped weeping and allowed him to help her through the doorway, into the makeshift infirmary. He would find mother and child a place out of the sun to rest and bring them water.

Lee Hatton envied Claude Hayes his rocklike calm in the face of a maddening routine. Day after day he rose before first light and helped to bury those he had tried so diligently to save the previous night. Hayes was not cursed with a physician's ego-involvement in success or failure. His only purpose at the camp was to make things easier for the refugees, and that's what he did. With intelligence, concern and a seemingly bottomless well of feeling.

The doctor smiled at the next patient in line. "How is your baby's cough, today?" she asked.

The cool, dry fingers that skillfully examined mother and child belonged not only to a trained surgeon, but a professional mercenary. Like her close friend Hayes, Lee Hatton was a member of an elite and highly paid paramilitary team known as the Soldiers of Barrabas. The covert work of the SOBs was, at best, part-time. Three to six missions a year left plenty of room for outside interests and enterprise. After the destruction of Hatton's estate on Majorca by units of Spetsnaz, Soviet Military Intelligence death squads, neither she nor Claude had a home. Or an identity. Spetsnaz believed them to be dead. The decision to come to Ethiopia had been a neutral one. Both had already put most of their considerable personal fortunes into food programs for African refugees; the time had come to put their persons into the work as well.

Mercenaries using blood money to save innocent people.

Using hands that killed to heal.

It was not the contradiction it seemed.

Neither Hatton nor Hayes were stereotypes: grinning, lantern-jawed freebooters with a lust to spill human blood and wallow in the spoils of war. Nor were they political mad dogs, out to make the world safe for their favorite brand of tyranny.

After years of drifting from service to service, war to war, Hayes had found a point to his life in Mozambique, where he had fought for no payment against the white Portuguese oppressors. His commitment had not been to Marxist Frelimo, but to the helpless individuals caught up by an accident of birth in the most corrupt and degrading colonial system on the planet.

Leona Hatton had led her share of other lives as well: CIA operative, battlefield surgeon, expert in deadly Escrima knife- and stick-fighting techniques. First and foremost she was a doctor. The oath she had solemnly taken in that regard meant more to her than anything. A strikingly beautiful woman, she wore her raven-black hair cropped short as a man's. Although she joked about this habit of hers, saying her father, the general, had always wanted a boy, the real reason for the severe haircut was to diminish her physical attractiveness, which it did from a distance. The image the doctor chose to present to the world was one of quiet, controlled physical and mental power. Unlike her inherited good looks, this control was all her doing.

Dr. Lee stared into the face of the next black woman in line. Though drawn from weeks, perhaps months of hunger, it was still a lovely face, the nose fine and narrow, the brow high, teeth even and white behind full, sculptured lips. Large, dark, heavy-lidded eyes radiated an intense and, to Lee Hatton's way of thinking, thoroughly inappropriate joy. Their expression, however, was not nearly as unsettling as the accompanying smile. It was the smile of a lioness.

"May I see your baby?" Lee asked, holding out her hands for the rag-wrapped bundle.

The Tigre woman seemed to understand. She unwound the muslin from the child's head and chest. "Deneke," she said, proudly displaying her son. "Deneke Walatta."

Dr. Lee stiffened. In this case no stethoscope examination was necessary. "Let me take him," she said, trying to coax the tiny corpse from the woman's grip.

It was impossible.

"Claude," Lee called in an even voice.

Hayes stepped from the infirmary, ducking his head to clear the low doorway. He saw the smiling woman holding her dead child. He had witnessed such a thing many times in the ten weeks they had been working at Barem. The necessary words were no easier for that.

"Mother, your son has passed away," he said in Tigre, opening his big, callused hands to take the child.

The woman jerked the baby back, pressing it tightly to her chest, covering it with a protective arm. She shook her head violently.

Hayes gently pulled aside an edge of the rag shielding the baby's head. He said, "Look at him. Please, look at him."

Esther Walatta stared down into the little face and, for the first time, really saw. She fell apart. Her arms trembled uncontrollably as Hayes drew the little body from its cocoon of muslin windings.

"We must bury him," Hayes said to her. "Come with me."

The sanity that had appeared so suddenly in the woman's eyes just as quickly vanished. A light winking out. Clutching the wadded-up rag to her chest she turned without a word and rushed into the crowd.

Lee shouted for the woman to come back, then started after her. Hayes stepped into the doctor's path.

"We've got to help her, Claude," she said.

"How? How can we possibly help her?"

She had no answer for that.

"There are too many others waiting," Hayes said.

The lineup for examinations was much longer now, stretching around the corner of the ramshackle building and melting into the camp's constantly shifting human mass. Every night Lee dreamed of these lines. Of row upon row of pleading, exhausted faces. Lines without end.

Dr. Lee Hatton swallowed the blistering pain welling in her throat and focused her full attention on the next starving mother and child.

ESTHER WALATTA RAN in a blind panic through the camp, treading upon her fellow refugees and their meager possessions. She did not hear the shouts and curses; she did not feel the blows of retaliation. She ran past them all, well beyond the outer limit of the camp, gasping as she raced up the side of a low hill. When she reached the top, her legs finally gave out; she dropped first to her knees, then her face. Hot dust drank her tears and muffled her shrill wailing.

At journey's start there had been six of them: Esther, her husband, Osman, and their four children. At the drought-ravaged ruin of their family farm, they had left behind Osman's parents who were too weak to travel. They had set off to the south with what little food they had, looking for help. The two oldest children had died of starvation the very first week. Her husband had died soon after, though not from hunger. It had happened in the afternoon. The Walattas were walking on a road with some other refugees when a MiG jet had suddenly appeared out of the middle of the sun, swooping down on them, shrieking low overhead as it strafed the road. Osman had shoved Esther and the two surviving children into a ditch. He did not make it to safety himself. Cannonfire blew him apart, not six feet from where his family lay huddled.

Esther walked only at night after that.

During the day, she and her children slept under cover, coming out at dusk to furtively search the hillside for edible blades of grass and plant roots. Twenty-seven days later she put her last daughter in the ground. She had covered the shallow grave with the heaviest stone she could lift to keep the hyenas from digging it up....

With her own hands Esther Walatta had buried almost all there was of her life. She could bury no more. She could not accept the fact that the terrible ordeal had been for nothing, that in spite of her courage and determination her family was destroyed. Face down in the dirt she sobbed an insane litany over and over. Her baby was only lost. Only lost. He couldn't have gone far. She would find him again. She had to find him again.

Esther pushed up from the ground. Below the hilltop was a crude dirt road, and beside it an army truck sat parked in the spotty shade of an acacia. A lone uniformed soldier leaned on the lowered tail-gate. Perhaps he had seen her baby?

Esther ran down to the road, but by the time she reached the olive drab truck, the soldier had disappeared. Not that it mattered.

Her heart bubbled over with joy.

She had found her son.

There, in the dirt in the shadow of the tailgate he lay uncovered, his little back curved toward her. Beside him was a coil of wire. When Esther lifted the baby the wire came too. She tried to pull it free, but only managed to remove a stiff little folded piece tied with a string. She quickly wrapped up both her baby and the tangled wire in the muslin rag and hurried away down the road. Everything was going to be all right, after all. She would find the help they needed elsewhere. They would begin their life again.

Esther began to sing softly to her strange, still child. She sang him the song of plenty.

THE ETHIOPIAN ARMY PRIVATE zipped up his fly and stepped out from behind the trunk of the acacia tree. He stifled a prodigious yawn with the back of his hand. He squinted up at the sun, idly scratched his ear. There was no reason to hurry. His sergeant had taken the other truck and gone back to the supply base to get more trip wire, leaving him to work on his own. In peace, for a change. The sergeant was a stickler for doing everything by the book, even when there was an easier way.

When the private ambled around the rear of the truck he stopped short. It was gone! He dropped to one knee and searched frantically under the tailgate. A low moan escaped his lips as he straightened up. He'd only left the damned thing untended for a minute. It was ready to be installed, too; he'd even removed the locking safety.

He grabbed his FN battle rifle and scrambled up onto the roof of the truck cab, scanning the terrain in all directions. There was no one in sight. Was he losing his mind? He hopped back down, set his gun against the wheel well and made a quick count of the canvas satchels in the bed of the truck. No, it was definitely gone. If he had followed proper installation procedure, staked the damned thing in position first, it never could have happened.

What was he going to tell his sergeant?

The private paced back and forth behind the truck. Then the answer came to him. He would say nothing about the missing gear. Pretend it was just another mistake by the supply corps. Those fools couldn't count to five without using their fingers, and counting to five meant taking one out of their noses.

The private heaved a sigh and sat back on the tailgate. As he did so, he noticed something he had missed before, something lying partially buried in the dirt at his feet: a cotter pin with cord attached. He picked it up, wound the cord around the pin and threw it all as far from him as he could.

Whether by accident or on purpose, the thief had done something very stupid. With both its safeties removed, an M-3 detonator was a decidedly touchy little bastard. And the touchy little bastard in question was correctly connected to a Claymore M-18A1 antipersonnel mine. If the thief so much as sneezed he was going to be in for an extremely unpleasant surprise.

2

Tablespoon in fist, Walker Jessup stared dolefully at his triple portion of chocolate *gâteau*. The monstrous wedge stood five layers high, each layer of dark, rich cake separated by a quarter inch of creamy butter-fudge icing. Beside the clear glass plate and paper doily bearing the *gâteau* was the topping—fresh whipped cream in a frost-beaded, stainless steel cruet.

He wanted it.

In the worst way.

But a bonfire raged in his huge belly, the heat and smoke of world-class indigestion roaring up his esophagus. Both body and soul in torment, Jessup reached into the inside jacket pocket of his white suit, took out a plastic bottle of thick greenish fluid and unscrewed the cap.

He was pouring himself a fourth heaping tablespoon when his waiter approached, very much alarmed. "Is something the matter, Mr. Jessup?" the black man asked.

Jessup powered down the medicine, gritting his teeth and shuddering at the taste. Something was wrong, all right, but it had nothing to do with the restaurant's cuisine or service. "I can't do the food justice tonight," he said sourly. "I'd like my bill, please."

The waiter visibly wilted. Not from fear of loss of tip but from loss of face. The fat American was a valued regular patron and usually an enormous eater. The waiter's unease was so pronounced that Jessup felt obliged to elaborate. "I've got a touch of heartburn from lunch at the hotel," he lied.

In point of fact, Walker Jessup's lunch had consisted of eight ounces of lime-flavored antacid. The Texan had been off his feed for days, a condition both rare and ominous. The last time Jessup missed a meal had been in Saigon, right before the fall.

The lie more than satisfied the waiter. "Perhaps you will take your lunch here tomorrow," the waiter suggested, without being too smug or too sympathetic. Honor restored, he marched back across the polished hardwood floor to his station against the whitewashed adobe wall. He stood between a pair of zebra-skin hangings and began adding up the tab for all the stuff Jessup had ordered and then only stared.

Jessup put the plastic bottle back inside his jacket. Over the strains of "My Way" coming from the bomba section of the restaurant, a garden patio covered by a thatched grass roof, he could hear the rumbling sounds of his stomach's discontent. It spoke truth to him.

He should have killed Karl Heiss on the dirt road in Sri Lanka. Shot the CIA renegade quick and cold and then ran a car over his head a couple of times to make sure he was dead. Or he could have just held the bastard for Barrabas. Only the devil knew what the white-haired man would have done to Heiss before he let him die. One thing was clear, Jessup hadn't made the right choice. He had made the smart choice. He had wanted to score points with his former employer, the CIA. He had agreed to handle a special, rush job: to save Heiss's life so the sleaze could perform an unspecified but "vital national security" function for the boys at Disneyland. This in return for also unspecified future favors. As operator of his own private intelligence service, Jessup relied heavily on traded favors with the big-budget guys, not just the CIA and the NSA, but their counterparts in France, England and Israel.

After the deed was done Jessup had had immediate second thoughts. Karl Heiss had been on the CIA's hit-on-sight list. Why would the CIA reinstate a known bad apple like Heiss? What kind of mission called for his particular talents? It had cost Jessup plenty to find out.

The CIA had made Heiss a silent partner in a TV preacher's enormously profitable Ethiopian famine-relief crusade. Heiss was supposed to loot the millions in charitable contributions, which then would be used by CIA to fund illicit operations. The CIA had chosen Heiss for the job because they knew he would pull a double cross. Heiss hadn't disappointed them. He had shown some initiative, too, first taking the TV preacher into his confidence, then investing relief funds in illegal drugs, using relief aircraft for drug smuggling.

What the CIA really wanted from Heiss was a scandal that would discredit the whole famine-relief movement, that would get all Western aid to Ethiopia cut off, forcing the Marxist government to try to cope with the disaster on its own, a task that would surely speed its collapse and the chance for a more friendly group to take power.

The end did not justify the means. The toll in suffering and human lives was going to be unthinkable. Even Jessup couldn't let it be.

He had paid more, in favors and cash, to wrangle a job as bagman on the mission, hoping to keep it from coming off as planned. In the past few days that hope had grown faint, at best. It looked more and more like he was going to be left holding the bag and that the bag was going to be empty. Walker Jessup was up to his chins in shit.

He paid the waiter in U.S. dollars and lumbered out of the restaurant, through the roofed garden, past its little piano bar, to the wrought-iron gate in the high adobe wall. The place was a converted private home, an upper-class residence on the outskirts of Addis Ababa. Jessup nodded to the gateman as he stepped through and onto the street beyond. High overhead, a quarter moon silver-edged the branches and leaves of the scrub acacia and eucalyptus that lined the narrow dirt road. It also lit up the road's deep ruts, a Grand Canyon in miniature.

The first in the short line of waiting taxis started up and crept forward, stopping beside him. The driver jumped out and opened the rear door for him. Like most of the cabs in Addis, it was small, a Fiat in this case, and beat to hell. It took some doing for the 350-pound man to wedge himself into the narrow back seat.

"Hilton," Jessup said.

The driver popped the clutch, sending the car lurching ahead, then hit the ruts at an angle.

"Damn!" Jessup growled as his head triple-thumped the roof. He clutched the back of the seat with one hand and jammed the other as hard as he could against the roof as the little car slewed and slithered, springs creaking mightily. There was about three-fourths of a mile of washboard to go before they hit the Airport Road and pavement.

Headlights suddenly lit up the dust-coated back window. A car was following closely with its high beams on. It gave Jessup the opportunity to see more than he wanted of the cab's interior. Seats ripped, cratered, upholstery foam granules everywhere. The driver used the dashboard to display his sizeable collection of cigar butts. Jessup tried to see out the side window, but what with the glare and the dirt he couldn't make out much. Out the front window, in the feeble light of the taxi's headlamps, he saw trees and vague outlines of grass-roofed farmhouses that were no more than shacks.

The tailgater swung to one side, but Jessup's driver ignored what appeared to be an attempt to pass, continuing to steer down the middle of the track.

"Hey, let the guy get around," Jessup said, half turning on the seat to look back.

Autofire split the night, a hail of slugs thudding into the Fiat's trunk lid. "Shit!" the fat man gasped as something slammed him hard in the left side of his chest. The pain was numbing. He ducked down as best he could, groping under his jacket, fingers finding sticky fluid oozing all down his shirtfront. For an instant he thought he was hit bad. Then he smelled lime. Antacid.

Panicked by the gunshots, the driver took his foot off the gas.

The wrong thing to do.

Jessup grabbed for his ankle holster as the cab slowed sickeningly. His hand closed on the neoprene grips of his hidden wheelgun, and the custom weapon came away from its ballistic nylon sheath smooth and fast. It had been dehorned, de-edged, its hammer spur bobbed to nothing. "Drive, you idiot!" he shouted at the cabby, bringing the pistol's bull barrel up level with the top of the front seat.

"The EPLF!" the man cried. "The guerrillas will kill us if we try to run!"

Jessup shoved the muzzle of the .44 Special into the base of the taximan's skull. He said, "Die now, or die later."

The driver floored it and cut hard left, tires spinning, aluminum four-banger screaming a quavering high "C."

More automatic gunfire cracked through the night. A couple of stray slugs shattered the left corner of the back window, whistling between Jessup and the driver, exiting through the right-front passenger side window. Then either the steering locked or the cabby froze up at the controls because the taxi bounded straight across the road, sliding nose first into a sewage ditch.

Because the driver still had the gas pedal mashed to the firewall, the cab didn't stop. It hurtled on at a seventy-degree angle, left-side wheels in the bottom of the ditch, right-side scrabbling at the edge of the road, undercarriage shrieking as it scraped over the raised lip of the ditch. After fifty feet the ditch deepened and the car ground to a halt, drive wheels spinning.

The cabby bailed out; Jessup followed as quickly as he could, crawling out of the passenger door, on hands and knees through the stinking ditch water and then up and running into dim, flat boondocks.

Bullets slammed tree trunks and gnawed branches on either side of the fat man. Wet splinters of green wood pelted him as he weaved, huffing and puffing, through the scrub. Two SMGs on his ass. On his all-white ass. In his ice-cream suit he was a perfect poor-light target, a beached Moby Dick. He couldn't run much farther, either. His shirt and pants were soaked through with sweat, his legs turning to mush with every step.

He burst into a little clearing in the brush, half-trampled a goat and then nearly fell over a cow that was sleeping on the ground next to a downed eucalyptus. It woke up, raised its head and looked at him, but it didn't get up. In the patchy shadow of the clearing it was practically invisible. Its hind end was huge, almost as big as his. Jessup stripped off his white coat and spread it over the cow's rear, then he took cover behind the fallen tree, the bulldog .44 in both hands.

Even though he was looking for them, he didn't see the men approach the clearing. There was no mistaking the orange muzzle flashes of their weapons, the canvas-ripping sound of sustained full-auto bursts. Jessup could feel the shock waves of the bullet impacts right through the ground. The cow felt much worse than that. As it absorbed multiple hits in the backside, it tried to get up, then collapsed with a horrible bellow. The would-be assassins stopped shooting and stepped cautiously into a pool of moonlight, silver-edged silhouettes half crouching thirty-five feet away.

Jessup fired double action from the steady support of the fallen tree trunk. Each twelve pounds of squeeze he put on the trigger unleased two hundred grains of mad-as-hell Silvertip. He squeezed five times and all five of the big, slow-moving hollow-points struck meat. It was like being run over by a semi in low gear. Both men went down hard and stayed down.

The only one thrashing was the cow.

Jessup dumped the empties and used a speed loader to reload. Crazy with fear and pain, the cow kept trying to get up; its spine shattered, it was never going to make it. Jessup shot it once in the middle of the forehead. His suit jacket was a write-off.

He walked cautiously over to where the two bodies lay on their backs. He noticed the weapons first. They were Czech Model 25 submachine guns. Maybe the driver had been right, he thought, maybe the bastards were EPLF, Eritrean guerrillas doing a little nocturnal fund-raising for their cause. Then he moved closer to the corpses. Their faces were white.

Not EPLF.

Heiss. Heiss, hedging his bets.

Jessup's stomach rumbled and churned. Talking truth. Outnumbered, outgunned, he couldn't handle things by himself any longer. He was going to have to call for help. Use his hole card: the SOBs.

There was one small problem, however. If Nile Barrabas, leader of the mercenary band, happened to find out that he had let Heiss escape in Sri Lanka on purpose, on assignment for the CIA, his hole card would also be his executioner.

3

Nile Barrabas licked rock salt from the web of his left hand, raised the liter bottle to his lips and drank through clenched teeth. Oily Oaxacan mescal trickling steadily down his throat. He swallowed until the hard little head of the *cusano* bumped against the front of his teeth, then lowered the bottle, letting the plump, pickled worm slip back into the inch of liquor that still remained. He found a fresh wedge of lime among the litter of green rinds on the bedside table and bit into it.

Mescal didn't work on him like ordinary booze. It didn't make him happy drunk at all. It made him fighting mad. It burrowed under his whole skin, burning there like an overdose of tropical sun. He washed the taste of the cactus liquor out of his mouth with a swallow of Tecate beer from a can. Then he took the crumpled telex from his pants pocket, flattened it out on the bed in front of him and reread it, tendons in his square, solid jaw flexing.

The hotel room's air conditioner clicked on, its fan clattering desperately until it reached cruising speed. Over the loud droning he could still hear the sound of breaking surf in the bay below the room's balcony. On the other double bed Erika lay sleeping on her stomach, the thin coverlet drawn haphazardly over her back, covering very little of her tanned, naked body. Long slender legs stuck out from under the sheet. She had painted her toenails bright red. Looking at them on her small, perfect feet made the white-haired man smile for a second, then the smile switched off.

The two weeks in the little provincial Mexican seacoast town of Zihuatanejo was supposed to have been an R and R for them both. A chance to steal some time of their own, to hide from the world, from everything that they were and everything they were not. After four days they both knew the idyllic holiday was over—over long before Jessup's telex arrived. It had never really gotten started.

He held the bottle of mescal up to the bedstand light and shook it, making the two-and-a-half-inch long, segmented worm tumble and dance among the greasy bubbles in the translucent yellow liquid.

Barrabas knew firsthand that life was an abrasive process, that nobody stayed the same, unless they were dead, pickled like *el cusano*. Erika Dykstra had been changed against her will. And for the worst. It wasn't noticeable to anyone who didn't know her well. The statuesque blond smuggler could still laugh and have a good time. But she had nightmares. Four or five times a night she woke up with a jolt, wide-eyed and trembling, sweating profusely. Barrabas had seen the symptoms before, had felt them himself. Combat flashback.

Erika had been in Vietnam during the war, that's where she and Barrabas had met. She and her brother, Gunther, Dutch nationals and civilian free-enterprisers, had smuggled weapons in and gold and art out. Her horror dreams came from a much more recent experience. An experience provided by Karl Heiss. In Sri Lanka, Heiss had held her captive, bait for a trap he had engineered for Barrabas. When everything had fallen apart, the SOBs about to overrun his fortress, Heiss had put a .38 Smith to Erika's head and pulled the trigger. He had wanted the pain to last, the pain for her and the pain for his old enemy, Barrabas, so he had aimed to miss. It worked.

Being that close to death had scared Erika in a way she had never been scared before. The ordeal had stolen something from her, her confidence, ease; it had made her brittle inside. But that was not the real problem. She would not let Barrabas help her through it. She had stared into the black, howling abyss and had finally seen what her lover, the mercenary leader was addicted to. And for the first time in their ten-year friendship, she was afraid of him.

Barrabas shut off the lamp and padded barefoot across the quarry-tile floor. He opened the door to the balcony and stepped out, bottle in hand. The humidity was tempered by a soft sea breeze. Boat lights reflected on the inky waters of the little bay. Stars glittered in profusion overhead. His face on fire, Barrabas drank the last of the mescal, letting the worm slip into his mouth. He rolled it around on his tongue.

Karl Heiss deserved to die for what he had done in Vietnam, for all the innocent, defenseless people he had sacrificed on his altar of greed; but he was going to die for what he had done to Erika.

Die slowly.

Die hard.

Die soon.

Barrabas bit down. The worm was soft, liquid under the tough, rubbery skin. He chewed, grinding his teeth, and the worm burst in his mouth, flooding it with a sickly sweet taste. He chewed until there was nothing left to chew.

Then he swallowed.

4

Liam O'Toole shook his head in disbelief. "What do you mean you won't sell my book?"

The owner of the tiny Bowery bookshop smiled weakly. "Sorry, but I'm overstocked on poetry."

"You *specialize* in poetry," O'Toole protested, gesturing first at the shabby, overloaded bookcases lining the walls, bookcases crammed helter-skelter with collections of verse, most of them paper-bound and flyspecked, then at stacks of similar volumes piled knee-deep on the floor. The place reeked of mildewed rhyme. "I *write* poetry," the stocky, red-haired man said, patting the cardboard box under his left arm. It contained fifty softcover copies of his first and only published work. He had paid for its printing himself.

The store owner shrugged and fastidiously began to clean one set of dirty fingernails with the other. He wore a vinyl porkpie hat on his head, a scraggly gray beard on what there was of his chin, a threadbare brown sweater on his bony torso and a veritable street map of broken veins on his nose.

"Take six copies," O'Toole said. "Just six."

The proprietor looked up from his toilet. "Sorry."

"What's wrong with my book?"

The Skid Row businessman's rheumy eyes narrowed. His patience had run out. He wanted to retire to the solitude of his back room, his stained sofa, his gallon jug of sauterne and his critical study of the latest edition of "Teenage Sunworshipper" magazine. Clearly the "poet" who stood before him was too hardheaded to take a simple "no" for an answer. "You want to know what's wrong? Okay I'll tell you," he said, snatching the sample copy from O'Toole's hand. "The cover for one thing. What the hell is that a picture of? A bunch of dead people? A black-and-white picture printed in shades of red of a bunch of dead people in a ditch."

"Friends of mine."

"And if the cover art doesn't make you throw up, the title is sure to."

O'Toole stared at the title. *Maggot Picnic*. Maybe it was a little strong.

The store owner opened the volume at random and began reading. "'Red muck-smeared faces, upturned, disembodied, lay gaping on a sanguine, stagnant, quicksand sea: islands of paradise for blue-black beetles; maternity wards for hairy-legged flies.'" He slammed the book shut, then waved it in O'Toole's face. "What *is* this shit?" he demanded.

"Vietnam."

The bookseller scowled at him. "Nobody in their right mind could write this vomit, nobody in their right mind would buy it. It should be outlawed. And you should be locked up." He tossed the book back to O'Toole. "Take your garbage and get the hell out!"

Normally Liam O'Toole had a very short fuse. If it had been the first time in recent weeks the professional mercenary, a former IRA bomber and ex-U.S. Army captain had been thrown out of a bookstore, he might have taken the rejection personally; he might even have done something typically violent and antisocial. But it wasn't the first time, by a long shot. In the fourteen days since he had received copies of his *Maggot Picnic* from the vanity publishing house, he had been ushered out of every other bookstore on Manhattan. The seedy Bowery shop was the last on the list.

"You have a nice day, now," Liam told the man. He did consider kicking over a couple of heaps of books on his way out, but decided it would only improve his decor and why do the jerk a favor?

After a stop at the nearest liquor store for two quarts of Bushmills, O'Toole headed back to his Greenwich Village hotel room, muttering to himself. He could, he supposed, always try hawking his work in the boroughs of Brooklyn or Queens. In his heart he knew that just wouldn't do. He wanted to make it where it counted, in the Big Apple or nowhere. After his work had been turned down by every New York publisher and agent, both legitimate and illegitimate, he had swallowed his pride and reached into his own pocket. He had self-published in order to preserve his poetry for posterity. Thanks to Nile Barrabas, and a string of six-figure missions with the SOBs, the expenditure was no hardship for him.

As O'Toole walked along, he thought about sneaking back into one of the big chain stores on Fifth Avenue, secretly slipping a copy of his book on the shelves, on the off-chance that someone might pick it up and read it. He could see himself getting caught in the act. He had made rather strong negative impressions on the managers of those particular stores; they would not soon forget his face. No, it was all too humiliating, he decided.

As far as O'Toole was concerned, a writer without a sense of personal dignity was no writer at all, was nothing better than a chimpanzee trained to thump a typewriter with fists and feet, a paper diaper under its Donegal tweeds. If reaching posterity meant wearing a monkey suit, then posterity could damn well go to hell.

He entered the hotel lobby, dropped his box of books and booze on the counter and asked for his room key. As the clerk turned to get it, a group of O'Toole's fellow tenants came out of the elevator.

There were two guys and two girls. All of them had six-inch-high mohawks: one was hot pink, one was crimson tipped with black, there was an all Day-Glo green, and a muddy rainbow. All had on motorcycle jackets, studded dog collars, leopard-skin tights and cowboy boots. Quadruplets, except for personal preference in hair color...and facial tattoos.

"You have a telex," the clerk said, handing it and the key to O'Toole.

Liam scanned the message. "Make up my bill," he told the clerk. "I'm leaving in ten minutes for JFK."

One of the punkers was looking into the cardboard box.

"Want a book?" Liam said.

The girl with the tattooed teardrop at the corner of her left eye showed the cover to her boyfriend, who had a little black spider tattooed beside his nose.

"Hell," O'Toole said, removing the Irish whiskey from the box. "Take 'em all. Compliments of the author." He shoved the box over to them.

The girl opened her mouth to say something. Liam didn't give her the chance to get it out. He headed for the elevator, his quart bottles clinking together. He'd endured more than enough rejection for one day. Besides, he had a plane to catch.

5

Pink neon sizzled in the stage's wraparound ebony mirrors, rock-and-roll thunder fading to a throbbing solo bass line. The blond topless dancer dropped to her back in time with the driving beat, lying down on the job. She raised, then scissored her impossibly long legs, framing her red-G-string-clad mound of Venus with the smooth backs of her thighs.

"Yaaaah-whoooooooo!" the all-male audience howled as she drew her legs even farther back, touching knee to shoulder.

Nanos the Greek, past his twentieth kamikaze and well into his fifth pitcher of beer, cupped a hand to his mouth and bellowed over the din of catcalls and whistles, "Holyeeeeeee-shit!" He and Billy Two were sitting at the padded counter, which was level with and ringed the perimeter of the stage, no more than four feet from the tiny triangle of red satin. They were the only two guys in the packed bar who weren't wearing baseball caps or cowboy hats.

The Greek glanced over at his old buddy and the wild enthusiasm on his face turned to an expression of concern. The six-foot-six-inch Osage Navajo was staring intently at the shiny little strip of costume, his lips moving, his words unintelligible over the noise.

Nanos nudged him with an elbow and said in his ear, "You having any fun?"

It was like talking to a tree stump.

The huge redman stopped mumbling and picked up the half-full pitcher of beer in front of him. He didn't bother with a glass; he drank from the jug.

"Thirsty work, huh?" Nanos said as his friend put down an empty pitcher. "We need more suds."

Billy Two didn't respond. His glassy, unblinking gaze was riveted elsewhere. The dancer had rolled over onto elbows and knees, arched her spine and was offering her svelte backside to an appreciative crowd.

Nanos waved at their waitress. He needed a lot more suds. Of late, William Starfoot II, a.k.a. Billy Two, had become a serious bring-down to him. They had been running buddies for years, long before they joined up with the SOBs, but since the Indian's stay in a Moscow "mental hospital" as a guest of GRU, Soviet Military Intelligence, he just wasn't the same guy. He was quiet when he should have been loud, loud when should have been quiet. He had gotten wierd in other ways, too. Billy Two had always been infected with the back-to-nature crap, part of his Native American fantasy life. Thanks to GRU's "treatments," fantasy had become reality. Nanos had practically dragged him from a primitive cabin in Fairbanks, Alaska, where he had set up housekeeping with "Noweena," a deceased friend's thousand-pound pet bear. Talk about odd couple!

The music crescendoed and stopped. The dancer took a few bows, put her floor-length red negligee back on, then made the circuit around the edge of the stage, picking up the tips the patrons had left on the counter for her. As she scooped up the money, she squatted down right in front of them, knees parted. When she squatted in front of Billy Two she opened her thighs extra wide.

Which started the redman mumbling again.

Nanos could hear it clearly now. He couldn't understand it, though. It was Indian talk, and from the rapturous look on Billy's face, it might be ardent words of love. The Greek was mightily relieved. His plan to bring Billy Two back to the real world by plunging him into familiar wallowing-grounds seemed to be having positive results. Better a bimbo than a beer.

The dancer gave the audience one last bow, tossing up the hem of her negligee, mooning them, then retired to the dressing room adjoining the stage to count her fistful of singles.

Billy Two stared at the closed dressing-room door as if trying to burn holes through it.

Then the waitress showed up with their fresh pitchers. As she set them down, there was a mass exodus of the bar's other customers.

"What's going on?" the Greek said.

"After 7:00 P.M. this place switches over to male dancers," the waitress told him as she made change.

"We'd better drink up, then," Nanos said.

"That's what all the guys do," the waitress said. "They don't know what they're missing."

"Huh?"

"Stick around for half an hour, you'll see."

Nanos gave her a doubtful look.

"Trust me," she said, winking at him.

As the waitress walked off, Nanos said. "You really want to stay, Billy?"

The Indian hoisted a pitcher to his lips and lowered its level by a good three inches.

"Hey, sure, pal, whatever you say," Nanos grumbled, sipping from the rim of his jug.

No sooner had the men trooped out of the bar, then the women trooped in. Women in business suits, in housedresses, in jeans. They must have been waiting in line outside. All were in excellent spirits, laughing, calling to each other as they rushed to get the choice seats around the stage.

The show was already starting. Lights flashed and the music cranked up. A guy in black leather pants stepped out on the stage. He was so casual, with his aviator's sunglasses propped on top of his head and a worn leather jacket slung over his shoulder, that it was almost painful.

"Chuck-eee!" one of the women shrieked.

Then they were all shouting the dancer's name. He blew them a kiss, then began to dance and take his clothes off at the same time.

Nanos knew a fellow bodybuilder when he saw one. Unlike the Greek, the guy on the stage wasn't all bulked up, massive slabs of interlocking gridwork. He had hard, wiry muscles, from lots of reps with no weight. He had a deep all-over tan and no body fat to speak of.

The woman to Nanos's left, a pretty brunet, early thirties, gray three-piece suit and tie, maybe a lawyer or bank exec, noticed and completely mistook his interest in the dancer's physique. She leaned against him and shouted over the music, "Hot stuff, huh?"

"A fucking wimp," was his reply.

As Chuck-eee got down to his black G-string, things began to loosen up. A woman in her mid-twenties practically climbed over Nano's back, shouting, waving a dollar bill in her hand. The dancer pumped his way to stage front and leaned forward, letting the lady stick the money in the front of his costume. She wasn't satisfied with just leaving a tip, though. Chuck-eee had to grab her hand by the wrist and forcibly remove it from inside his G-string.

Which made the crowd squeal with delight. They weren't much different from the men; they just did their yelling in a higher key.

"I suppose," the lady attorney continued, belligerently, "that you could do it better?"

Nanos looked aghast. "No, not me," he told her. He indicated Billy Two with a thumb. "My buddy, he's a regular dancing machine."

The redman, bored with Chuck-eee's stage act, had been leering over at the prim brunet for the past couple of minutes. His lips were moving soundlessly.

"She wants to see some of your natural rhythm," Nanos told him.

"Yeah, I do," the woman said.

Billy frowned at the guy cavorting on the stage.

"Chuck-eee needs a break," Nanos said.

As the music changed and the Temptations's "Ain't Too Proud To Beg" started blasting from the wall speakers, Billy Two scrambled up on the stage. The audience didn't know what to do at first, some of them cheered, some booed. Chuck-eee stopped prancing and put up a facade of outrage. It lasted two seconds. When he saw how big the Indian was and how obviously crazy, the dancer took off for the fire exit, leaving his clothes behind.

Billy Two faced the audience. "You want to see it?" he hollered.

"Strip! Strip!" came the chant.

The ladies sitting at the stage's rim started pounding on the counter, making the ashtrays and glasses jump. Nanos was laughing so hard his cheeks ached.

Billy got down to his jockey knits in record time. Mr. Natural. His coppery tan was permanent and though he had never pumped iron in his life, he had the broad-shouldered, narrow-hipped shape that bodybuilders go through hell to achieve. He had no fat, anywhere. When he swung his arms to the music the sinews and ligaments underneath the solid musculature of his chest jerked like steel cables. To the beat of the Temps he did a kind of hopping war dance, interspersed with violent pelvic thrusts.

The girls ate it up.

"What a stud!" gushed a steno-typist, standing on Billy's vacated chair.

Women rushed the stage, en masse, waving money. Billy danced in place, letting them stuff away. His jockey knits bulged with dollar bills. Then the brunet sitting next to Nanos gave a howl and jumped up on the stage with the others. She shoved a hundred dollar bill in the Indian's face. Then she shoved it and her hand inside his shorts.

"What're you trying to do, make change?" Nanos yelled, tears of laughter rolling down his cramped cheeks.

Whatever she was doing in there, it made a change come over Billy Two. A change obvious to anybody with eyes.

The ladies went berserk, shrieking, dancing on tables, throwing coins at the stage, throwing their drinks at each other.

The brunet in the three piece, Billy Two firmly in hand, faced the rioting audience and pulled a flat wallet from her coat pocket. She let it fall open, displaying a big silver badge. "This is a raid! You are all under arrest!" she cried.

On cue, the exit doors burst inward and uniformed, baton-wielding male and female officers rushed in.

Nanos just sat there, stunned. He let a lady cop half his size twist his arm behind his back and lock it there with two feet of heat-treated club.

"Try anything funny, tough guy," she said as she bent him over a table, "and I'll break it off."

"This isn't really happening," Nanos moaned.

FOUR HOURS LATER the charges on the Greek were dropped and he was released. When he swung by their motel room to get the cash for Billy's bail bond, he was handed the telex from Barrabas.

It was almost three in the morning by the time the two SOBs were back on the street. Billy Two looked infuriatingly rested for his experience.

Nanos showed the Indian the message. "We got to go, today," he said.

"Jump bail?"

"Too bad you can't stick around and fight the charges. You'd win for sure. I've never seen a clearer case of entrapment. That undercover cop had you right where she wanted you."

The Indian grinned. "Entrapment, hell! Another minute and I would've proposed to her."

The Greek beamed at his old friend. Things were *finally* getting back to normal.

6

Walker Jessup answered the knock at his hotel-room door. When he opened it he found himself staring right into the face of Nile Barrabas. A face hewn of stone. From below heavy lids, the ex-Army colonel's cool cobra eyes seemed to skewer his very soul. Jessup quickly broke contact, looking past the man's shoulder. In the hall on the other side of Barrabas were three of his SOBs: Alex Nanos, William Starfoot II and Liam O'Toole.

O'Toole was wearing a gaudy Aloha shirt, baggy white pants and a big grin. Probably drunk out of his tiny mind, Jessup thought sourly. After all it *was* nine-thirty in the morning. Among the bums and boozers known collectively as the Soldiers of Barrabas, Jessup considered ex-U.S. Army Captain Liam O'Toole the unqualified weakest link.

"Come in, come in," Jessup said, stepping aside. "The others are already here."

Dr. Lee Hatton and Claude Hayes rose from the couch to greet their comrades.

"Good to see your ugly faces again," the doctor said.

Nanos seized the opportunity to draw the lovely lady into his arms. "Hey, I can feel your bones!" Nanos exclaimed as he gave her a friendly squeeze.

"Down, Alex," she told him, untangling herself from the hug.

"You on a crash diet, or something?"

Hayes answered the Greek's question for her. "Yeah, it's a crash diet, all right. We've both been living on the same rations the refugees get."

"We heard that you two were working over here," O'Toole said. "Is it as bad as the press makes out?"

"Worse," the doctor said. "Believe me, Claude and I wouldn't have left the people at the camp if Jessup hadn't convinced us that our services were required here in Addis for something much more important over the long haul."

"Let's get down to it," Barrabas told the fat man as he and the other SOBs took seats around the room, on chairs, couch and the bed. "Where's Heiss?"

"Over at government house," Jessup said. "He and his partner are trying to bribe the Dergue into letting them shoot a live-satellite TV spot at a refugee center in the north. I have to put in an official appearance over there this afternoon, too."

"What's the scam?" the mercenary leader demanded.

Jessup loosened his tie and unbuttoned his collar. Then he began to talk very fast. "Two months ago the CIA arranged for Karl Heiss to become a half partner in the 'Lalarva Crusade '85.' It's a pseudoreligious, money-collecting machine, the creation of Dr. Tuttle Lalarva of Studio City, California. He's a preacher with his own syndicated cable TV show. Dr. Lalarva had big problems with the Feds, and the IRS in particular. He was taking in charity money hand over fist and none of it was going out. To escape a Federal indictment for mail fraud, he agreed to cooperate with the CIA and let Heiss into the business. The preacher thought Heiss was supposed to make sure the money got distributed here in Ethiopia. Actually, he was supposed to steal it for the CIA. After looking over the operation, Heiss decided he had a better idea. He told the preacher about the CIA's plan to rip him off and then sold the guy on a whole new thrust. They would bring the charity money over here, spend a little of it for show, but use the bulk of it to buy heroin and cocaine, use Crusade '85 airplanes to transport the stuff. You remember, Heiss had all those Golden Triangle connections from the Nam days."

"I remember," Barrabas said. "How much do you figure he's stolen?"

"I know for a fact that he's got thirty million dollars cached away here in Addis."

"Holy shit!" said the Greek.

"It's all in hundred-dollar bills," Jessup went on, "packed away inside fifty-kilo grain sacks."

"How many sacks is that?" O'Toole asked.

"A dozen."

"What exactly is your part in the deal?" Barrabas said.

"I'm supposed to get the cash to a CIA-operated bank on Antigua. The move is scheduled to come off this week, but Heiss has no intention of letting it happen. He turned a couple of his hired hands loose on me two days ago. My execution was supposed to look like an attempted robbery."

Billy Two leaned over and whispered to Hayes, "How'd they miss a target *that* big?"

The black man shrugged. "Maybe they mistook him for an aircraft hangar?"

"I think Heiss is going to try and move the money out of the country in the next twenty-four to forty-eight hours," Jessup said. "The shooting of this live fund-raiser could just be a ploy to get travel passes into Eritrea. From there it's only a short hop to the Sudan. And anything can happen in the Sudan these days."

"How many in the opposition?" Barrabas asked.

"He's got twenty men, now. All experienced mercs. Typical Heiss trash. Rejects from armies of the west. The money is stored in a former embassy on the road to the airport. It's completely walled in, set to hold off everything but an air strike.''

''You got a scale map?'' Barrabas asked.

Jessup took a folded paper from his shirt pocket and handed it to the white-haired man. ''I've marked the hard defensive positions in red.''

O'Toole peered over Barrabas's shoulder at the crude sketch. ''Twenty guys aren't going to be a problem if we do this right,'' he said. ''Let's hear the rest of it.''

''Security inside the city was set up for the Dergue by the East Germans. The communications system here is terrible, where it exists at all, but once the security forces get rolling they are as efficient as hell. If our operation in and out takes longer than fifteen minutes, we'll be dead. I almost forgot to mention the dogs.''

''Dogs?'' Lee said.

''The grounds are also guarded by dogs.''

''Like in those Ethiopian dog jokes?'' Nanos said. ''You know, what is an Ethiopian walking two dogs? A caterer.''

''Real unfunny,'' Dr. Hatton said.

''Do you know how they train their guard dogs over here?'' Hayes asked him. ''They cage them up from the age of six weeks, feed them irregularly and pay a stranger to come over and beat them with a stick a couple of times a day. They're always kept chained up. Man's best friend, my ass! You want to see an Ethiopian piss his pants? Unchain his dog and let it loose in the house.''

''We aren't going to take this place, dogs and all, with our bare hands, I trust?'' O'Toole said.

''The armament's all arranged. Your weapons are waiting in a warehouse near here. Directions are on the other side of the sketch map. I got you a pair of heavy barrel FN FALs and .308 armor-piercing ammunition, four 9 mm Heckler and Koch MP5 SD3 submachine guns with factory silencers, and for everyone, 9 mm Beretta Model 925B sidearms, also suppressor-equipped.''

''What are we going to do with the loot after we capture it?'' Billy asked.

''Make the biggest private cash donation in history. We drive the money onto the grounds of the Swiss embassy and park it. The International Red Cross can take it from there.''

''Will the Swiss handle our exit from Ethiopia?'' Barrabas asked.

''Only if we have Heiss or the military in hot pursuit right up to the embassy gates. Otherwise we're going to have to rely on my organization to get us out.''

''Hayes and I aren't leaving,'' Dr. Hatton said. ''Once we're done in Addis, we go back to the aid station in the north.''

Hayes nodded.

"Suit yourselves," Jessup said.

Barrabas had turned to face the hotel room's large window. Seven stories below, tin-roofed, plywood-walled slums jammed right up against the Hilton's multimillion-dollar security fence. Beyond the shacks was a cow pasture doubling as a soccer field. A pick-up game was in progress, the players passing the ball between the legs of grazing livestock. Barrabas gazed down on the city and saw none of it. He was still looking at the map of the kill zone. It was etched into his brain.

"O'Toole," he said, turning back to the others, "you and I will plan the assault this afternoon. We'll hit the place hard, tonight." He stared at Jessup for a moment, then said, "Are you going to fight alongside us or just lead the cheering section, as usual?"

The fat man was sweating rings under the arms of his short-sleeved dress shirt. "I wouldn't miss this one for the world," he said, grabbing his sport coat. "I've got to go, now. I'll meet you at the warehouse around 8:00 P.M. The key to the warehouse door is in the ashtray on the nightstand with a room key. If you need anything else, ring room service. Don't leave the hotel during daylight. Addis is crawling with Soviet and Cuban advisors."

After he had hurried out the door, Liam said, "You know, I think Jessup would miss it, if he could."

"The question is, how did he get in it in the first place?" Barrabas said. "You noticed he didn't bother to explain that to us."

"You're absolutely right, Colonel," Hayes said. "This deal was dirty from the beginning. If Jessup was acting as a CIA bagman, he had to know the whole story. This guy doesn't lift a finger unless he has all the answers."

"Yeah, the fat man's dirty, all right," O'Toole said with conviction.

"You'd better follow him, Liam," Barrabas said.

"You read my mind, sir." O'Toole turned and made a quick exit.

Barrabas again faced the hotel-room window, grimacing at his own faint reflection in the glass. What the hell had he gotten his people into?

7

The Dergue hearing was human interaction at its most primitive. To find a truly apt parallel, Karl Heiss had to strain his memory, dredging up lessons in ancient history from his Harvard days. He decided the hearing compared favorably to a royal audience, circa 1200 A.D. The setting was much different, of course. Instead of a drafty stone castle, it was an overheated federal auditorium. And the royalty at center stage, high above the crowd, were not seated on thrones, but folding chairs behind a folding table; clad not in lavish finery but khaki. Four black princes in military-issue shirts, shorts, socks, boots, field caps.

Heiss regarded them with amused contempt. The judges of the Dergue were as pompously ignorant as any medieval monarch. Their court was bedlam. Silver microphones atop their table squealed feedback. Soldiers armed with flat-back, Soviet-made assault rifles ringed the stage, holding back suppliants who stood shoulder to shoulder, waving pieces of paper at the grim-faced men on the platform.

They sought favors, not justice, dispensations for minor infractions of revolutionary law, signatures for desperately needed permits.

What with the clamor, the stale air, the bright jumble of native costume, the sheer confusion, the proceedings had an undeniable element of carnival.

Carnival Macabre.

The show in Ethiopia had been running nonstop since 1978, when Mengistu Haile Mariam, along with one hundred twenty other illiterate soldiers, seized power and formed the Dergue or "committee" to rule the newborn Marxist state. Mengistu made himself president. Of the original Dergue members only forty had survived the postrevolutionary bloodbath.

Social Darwinism.

Retroactive abortion.

Karl Heiss laughed aloud.

If Heiss thoroughly enjoyed the spectacle, the comedy of Third World politics, the man sitting beside him on the hard wooden bench did not.

Dr. Tuttle Lalarva stank of fear.

Heiss wrinkled his nose and glared at his business partner. Lalarva wore purple-tinted, frameless eyeglasses, the kind of glasses a car salesman or a professional bowler would choose. The kind of glasses that worked well with a leisure suit or safari jacket. Behind the subtly curved lenses, Lalarva's eyes never stopped moving; they darted this way and that, taking in everything, seeing nothing. His pudgy, dimpled, all-American face glistened with a patino of oily sweat; his dark blond hair, a sleek, razor-cut pompador, had begun to come unsprayed. Heiss knew that Dr. Tuttle Lalarva yearned to be back in his own element, the San Fernando Valley or its geo-cultural equivalent, someplace where the cops operated within the bounds of reason, never stomping the shit out of anybody white who owned a 450-class Mercedes.

From the start Heiss had sized Lalarva up as a chickenshit bastard. The preacher had neatly shorn his video flock, all right. He had collected millions in contributions to his fraudulent "crusade." But he had been afraid to take the money and run. Afraid to take that first irreversible step. Lalarva was a man with limited vision, in every sense, but he had plenty of luck. He had been in the right place at the right time with his cable TV show. Touching on the right guilt.

A terrible commotion erupted behind them.

Heiss craned his neck in time to see the auditorium's double doors crash open. A film crew, cameras rolling, floodlights glaring, pushed into the packed room. The spotlights transfixed a small, pale young man with a strange haircut, part long, part short, all of it bristling. As the cinematic phalanx bullied its way through the crowd, the young man gesticulated wildly at the black men up on the stage, pointing an accusing finger. The armed soldiers automatically closed ranks, shouldered their AK-47s and took aim.

"Who is that?" Lalarva exclaimed.

Heiss had seen the kid at hearings before. "Some kind of rock star," he said.

The rock star harangued the Dergue's judges. "I have a whole planeload of grain sitting out there on the airport runway," he told them. "I bought it. I paid for the transportation here. I'm ready to deliver it to the starving refugees myself. You people won't give me permission to take off. I want, no, I demand an immediate explanation!"

The three cameras rolled on, taking shots of both the singer and the stage, capturing his tirade and the initial, self-conscious reactions of the Dergue members as they realized they, too, were being filmed.

Major General Asrat, the bearded senior member of the board, shielded his eyes from the powerful floodlights. "Your case is still under review, Mr. Smooth. You will be duly notified of our final decision."

Smooth, born Horace Earl Smith in Launceston, Cornwall, England, refused to be put off. "People are dying out there!" he yelled furiously. As he did so, the cameraman kneeling in front of him zoomed in for an extreme close-up of his pasty, pitted face and his wildly upsprouting hairdo. "You don't care about your own people! What kind of government are you? What kind of world is this! All I want to do is to deliver the food, dammit!''

"If you and your companions don't leave the auditorium at once," the major general said into the microphone, his booming, amplified voice deadly calm, "I will order the guards to open fire.''

"Guns! Guns!" the singer ranted. "That's all you understand.''

There was a long moment of impasse, rock star and major general staring each other down while camera motors hummed. Everyone in the hall held their breath. The tension-packed stillness shattered when a stage mike let loose a piercing howl of feedback.

One of the entourage waved his arms overhead exhuberantly. "Cut! Cut! Got it! Great! Everybody was just great! Smooth, you were super!" he shouted. "That's a definite wrap!''

Lalarva shook his head in disbelief. "What is going on here?" he groaned.

Heiss watched the crew troop for the exit. Just as they reached it, the doors swung inward and a huge man lumbered into the room. The collision was immediate. One of the crew backed into the onrushing mountain and, conceding some two hundred pounds in weight, ended up flat on his face on the floor. The thin sheaf of papers the crewman had been holding under his arm shot straight up in the air, then fluttered slowly down, scattering far and wide.

The fat man made no attempt to help the fallen guy to his feet.

Heiss knew why. If Walker Jessup had tried to bend over that far, he would've ended up on his face, too. Heiss fumed inwardly. How could someone so blatantly out of shape have managed to escape a hit by seasoned professionals? No, not just escape, but turn the tables on them! Heiss had seriously underestimated the fat man's ability to defend himself. He would not make the same mistake again.

The crowd helped gather up the sheets of paper, passing them back to the crew as they got their man up from the floor. Then the crew left. After the doors shut a boy shoved a sheet of paper into the fat man's hand, thinking he was part of the filming. He looked at it, shrugged and shuffled over to where Heiss and Lalarva sat, all smiles. If he connected the attempted hit to Heiss, he was too smart to let it be known.

"What have you got there?" Heiss asked.

Jessup handed him the page. "Beats me."

Heiss scanned the first couple of lines, grinned, then read them aloud for the preacher's benefit. "I bought it. I paid for the transportation here. I'm ready to deliver it to the starving refugees myself."

"A script?" Lalarva said.

"They're shooting a music video," Heiss said. "I don't think the major general has the slightest idea what's going on, or how he's being used."

A uniformed soldier crooked a finger at Lalarva, Heiss and Jessup, indicating that they all should approach the stage.

As the trio moved through the mess of people, Lalarva warned Heiss, "For God's sake, don't mention the video. We want Asrat in a good mood."

The guards parted ranks, permitting them to mount the steps. As they crossed the stage's creaky wooden floor, the major general reached out and pointedly turned off his microphone. His colleagues quickly followed suit.

A closed session.

"Good morning, Major General," Heiss said. "Have you made a decision on our application for travel permits?"

The bearded black man frowned at the lieutenant to his left. "You have the paperwork, Hailu?"

Lieutenant Hailu shuffled through a stack of file folders, pulling out a thick one. He opened it and presented it to his superior.

Major General Asrat scanned through the topmost documents, then looked at the three white men in turn. "I fail to see the need for you to visit camps in disputed territory. Surely one of the locations closer to Addis would work just as well. After all, starving people all look much the same."

"It's a question of my supporters in the United States seeing exactly where their money is going," Lalarva said. "We have had some difficulties with overseas disbursement in the past. This will be a live satellite telecast from one of the Crusade '85 camps, the first of its kind. We will be introducing our contributors to the very people their donations will save, letting the unfortunate individuals tell their own, true stories of hardship and suffering. We believe that our friends in America will be moved by that living truth to further, even more warm-hearted acts of generosity."

Heiss noticed that the preacher's chin was starting to quiver with emotion. His talent for weeping at will was a regular feature on the TV show.

Asrat wasn't impressed.

"The problem, if you insist on visiting the north," the major general said, "is that I can't let you go without an official armed escort." He paused for effect. "And I do not have the surplus funds to apply to such an operation."

The good old squeeze, Heiss thought, fighting the urge to smile. That's why he loved the hell holes, the down and dirty places so much. Everything, everyone was for sale.

"I think there has been a misunderstanding," Heiss told the panel. "The Lalarva Crusade '85 is prepared to pay for all expenses incurred in the process of making its television messages. Did you have a figure in mind?''

The major general picked up a pencil and scribbled on the inside of the file folder. He then turned the folder around on the table so the trio could read it.

A pitiful sum.

Heiss feigned shock. Actually, he was reassured. If the Dergue had known about the plan to skip out with the whole bankroll, the major general's bribe would have been six figures instead of four.

After a short, suitably harried conference with his associates, Heiss accepted Asrat's demand. ''A bank draft will be cut as soon as we leave. Shall we make it out to the Dergue?''

''Make it out to me,'' Asrat said. He signed the travel passes and pushed them across the table.

''Where will we meet our escort?'' Heiss asked.

''They will meet you.''

''I take it, then, we're not to wait for them?''

Asrat eyed him humorlessly. ''That is correct.''

Heiss's suspicions were confirmed. There would be no armed military escort. It was just an excuse to cover the major general's extortion.

''Thank you,'' Lalarva said.

Their audience over, the three of them were escorted off the stage. Once they were in the corridor outside the auditorium, Lalarva said, ''Do you think the Dergue is on to us? What if they are just waiting for us to make a move with the money? Maybe we should call the whole thing off? Maybe we should wait until we're sure?''

"They don't suspect a thing," Heiss said.

"I agree," Jessup added. "If the Dergue suspected anything, they would've shut the operation down, confiscated everything a long time ago."

Lalarva grimaced, clearly unconvinced.

"Not to worry, Tuttle," Heiss told him. "Trust me, we're as good as home free." He winked at Walker Jessup. Who was as good as dead.

8

Major General Asrat turned on his microphone and curtly announced the hearing closed. As he pushed his chair back from the table, he ordered the troops to clear the hall. The decibel level doubled as citizens who had had no opportunity to put their cases to the panel raised their voices in angry protest. The guards answered protest with metal-shod rifle butts, driving the crowd backward and out the open exit doors.

As the tumult subsided, Asrat called his lieutenant aside. The bearded officer took a pair of cigars from his shirt pocket and offered one to the younger man.

"Thank you, sir," Hailu said, accepting the gift.

Asrat bit the end off the Havana and spit it on the floor. Then he stuck the cigar in the corner of his mouth. They were alone on the stage, the other two officers already crossing the auditorium floor, on their way out. "We have reason to celebrate," Asrat said. "You heard?"

The lieutenant nodded as he struck a paper match and held it to the end of his superior's cigar. "The preacher said, 'I want my supporters to know exactly where the money is going.' Do you think Heiss caught the tip-off?"

Asrat puffed away until the tip was a glowing coal and his head enveloped in a cloud of smoke. "I was watching his face. There was no reaction. Heiss knows nothing."

"If he had any suspicions, your asking for five thousand dollars certainly calmed them."

"A stroke of genius, if I do say so myself." Asrat's eyes narrowed. He didn't like having to say it himself. That's what he kept Hailu around for.

"Yes, sir," the lieutenant agreed emphatically, "a definite stroke of genius."

"They will try to move the cash tonight. By tomorrow morning I will be the richest man in Addis."

"Unless the preacher somehow betrays us."

"To whom? There is only Heiss. And it was his fear of Heiss that brought him to us in the first place."

"He could still change his mind at the last minute."

Asrat shook his head. "For the preacher I am the lesser of two evils. He might think there is a chance I will kill him after I liberate all the cash, but he knows for certain Heiss will do it."

"Did he really weep when he confessed the plan?"

"Like a woman," Asrat said in disgust.

Hailu lit his own cigar. "With my share I'm going to buy seven country nieces," he said, pausing to blow a plume of smoke aloft. "One for each day of the week. All of them very young and very pretty. And after a month or so, when I am tired of them, I will send them all down to the enlisted men's barracks and buy myself seven more."

"If you want seven pretty girl slaves, you're going to have to earn them," Asrat told him. "The preacher and I agreed that I would take twenty-five million for myself. No matter what happens, that money is mine. Should Lalarva die somehow during the operation, his five million is up for grabs."

Hailu said nothing. For a slice of five million dollars he would kill a thousand white preachers, ten thousand. For ten million all his own, he was going to kill a black major general.

"See to it that my special squad is ready and in place by eight-thirty this evening. I want that ambush site triple checked for security before I join them. Is that clear?"

"I'll get right on it, sir," Lt. Hailu said, saluting and hurrying off the stage, cigar tightly clenched between his teeth. There was no denying he had plenty to do before nightfall. He had two ambushes to arrange.

9

Jessup stepped out of the government building's lobby and onto the broad avenue. It was purple evening. In gigantic Revolution Square a block away, green, yellow and red Ethiopian flags furled in the breeze; enormous poster-likenesses of Marx, Lenin and Engels gazed down from high scaffolding, giving a perpetual socialist blessing to the heavy auto traffic below.

The fat man was in no mood for the Three Bearded Wise Asses. He gave them his own benediction, an up-raised middle finger. A couple of black male passersby turned to stare at him. They didn't know what the gesture meant; they knew from the suffused color of his face it was unfriendly. Jessup didn't give a damn.

He kept hearing Heiss's last words to him, seeing that smarmy wink. The wink had said, "I got you Jessup, your ass is mine anytime I want it." If it hadn't been for the armed soldiers in the auditorium the fat man would've drawn on Heiss then and there and killed the smug bastard on the spot. But a suddenly drawn gun in that room would've attracted hundreds of rounds of ammunition. Jessup was mad, but he wasn't crazy.

He grimaced and put a hand to his belly. It felt like he had swallowed a twelve-volt battery. A leaky twelve-volt battery. He took out his antacid and, forgetting about the spoon, chugged it straight from the bottle. He put the bottle back in his pocket and moved to the edge of the curb, waving impatiently at the biggest taxi in sight. Small taxis, particularly VW beetles, were the bane of his existence. He could get in, all right, but getting out was always a two-man job.

The cab in question, a battered Mercedes 220 diesel slashed across traffic, swerving for the curb from four lanes out. Before it could pull up alongside him, another car, a four-door, dark brown BMW cut in front. It stopped at the curb with squealing tires, both of its right-side doors flew open.

Jessup took an involuntary step back as two white men hopped out toward him, their right hands inside their unzipped cotton Windbreakers. He recognized them both as men in the employ of Heiss. He started to kneel, his hand dropping for his concealed weapon.

Something hard jammed under the bottom of his right shoulder blade. He froze in midcrouch.

"Get in the car," a voice behind him said.

Jessup hesitated. The ankle-holstered bulldog .44 was only a quick grab away. Quick was the operative word.

"Don't even think about it," the man behind him said, grinding the gun muzzle into his back. "In the car."

The guy who'd gotten out of the back seat returned the way he had come, backing in, a wicked grin on his face. As Jessup squeezed through the car doorway, across the rear bench seat, the fellow pulled a 9 mm Star M-30 PK from his belt, thumbed back the hammer and put the cold muzzle to the center of Jessup's forehead. The car's springs groaned as a third man got in the back and pulled the door shut. It was the guy who had come up behind him. Jessup knew this one by name. Leon. Leon held a .45 Colt Government Auto in his hairy hand. A real wildass, he had deactivated the grip safety by wrapping the grip with adhesive tape. The .45 was cocked and unlocked and resting against Jessup's right temple.

"Keep both your hands on your knees. If you move them the littlest bit, I'm going to shoot and then Ralphy's going to shoot. Got it?"

Jessup put his hands on his knees and kept them there.

"Drive!" Leon said.

The BMW pulled away from the curb and merged with traffic.

It was real close quarters in the back seat.

"Jesus, this guy even smells fat," Ralphy said.

"You messed up two of our pals the other night," Leon told the captive.

The guy in the front passenger seat turned and blew Jessup a kiss. "We're gonna mess you up even worse."

Jessup didn't say anything. He couldn't move his head what with the gun muzzles jammed against his skull from opposite sides. He could see the city sliding by, feel the last numbers of his life falling. He was going to get one or two before they got him. He would make his move after they got out of Addis, when they pulled off into the boonies to do the deed.

They didn't go that far.

The BMW turned instead into the Mercado, a compressed hodgepodge of native shops and dwellings, roughly ten square miles of densely populated city center. A good portion of that population ambled slowly down the middle of the narrow, winding street, forcing the car into a crawl. The street was lined with tiny, awning-shaded shops of all types, tourist traps selling phony African souvenirs, vegetable and fruit stands, machine shops, jewelers, junked auto parts and clothing stores. All of them wedged, crammed sideways into crumbling hovels of buildings. The tour buses only hit the outskirts of the Mercado. It wasn't safe to explore its heart, even in a large group. Jessup looked at the mildly curious brown and black faces staring through the car windows at him. They could see the guns at his head. They seemed, if anything, faintly amused at his plight. Jessup could expect no help from them. He had the feeling that the execution of a fat white man in the middle of the street would probably bring a round of applause. And shouts of "Encore!"

Then the BMW stopped.

LIAM O'TOOLE knew he had blown it when he saw the brown car screech up to the curb, saw the doors open and the men scramble out. Out of position, unarmed, he could only watch in silent fury as the guy stepped up behind Jessup to cut off his retreat, then forced him into the BMW.

As the car roared away from the curb O'Toole jumped into the front passenger seat of the Mercedes taxi that the BMW had cut off. "Follow that car!" he shouted at the driver.

The driver seemed to like the idea. He floored it, leaving behind a swirling fog of diesel exhaust.

"Can't you go any faster?" O'Toole snarled as the gap between the two vehicles widened. If they lost the BMW, Jessup was out of luck. Then the kidnap car turned right, off the main street and into the Mercado. Four other cars made the same turn before the Mercedes taxi. The cabby pulled in at the

tail end of the slow-moving line. It was like a goddamn funeral procession.

"Damn, I can walk faster than this!" Liam said.
With that he snatched a couple of bills out of his
pocket and threw them at the driver as he jumped
out of the rolling cab.

It was true. He could walk much faster than the
auto traffic. With difficulty he controlled the urge
to run alongside the BMW. When the cars stopped,
he stopped, pretending to look at junk jewelry or
pyramids of cabbages. The Mercado seemed to
stretch on forever before him, an endless maze, but
O'Toole knew it stopped eventually and that he had
to make his move before the BMW got out the other
side.

He counted four men beside Jessup in the car. He
could see the guns they were holding at the fat men's
head. What "move"? There was no way he could
get Jessup out alive. As he sidestepped, giving
ground to a man leading a cow on a rope, the BMW
swung over against the side of a building on the left
and stopped. To keep from blocking the following
traffic, it had to park so close to the wall that the
driver's side doors could not be opened. The guys
with guns made no attempt to conceal them as they
got out the passenger side, then made Jessup get
out. He watched them lead the fat man away.

O'Toole muttered a foul, multisyllabic curse under his breath. If he'd had anything to fight with he

could've made his play. He had to get some weapons and fast. Something in the shop front across the way caught his eye. Why the hell not, he asked himself.

JESSUP'S VOW to go down swinging stuck in his throat like a golf ball as a gun barrel pressed the back of his head. Another burrowed deep into the soft expanse of his belly. Heiss's men weren't giving him an inch of slack to work with. They quick-marched him around a crumbling corner. Overhead, across the eight-foot-wide gap of unpaved street between three-story buildings, clotheslines were strung. The mercs herded Jessup into a hole-in-the-wall tire repair shop; from the curt discussion that preceded the move, it had apparently been chosen at random. The entry was so narrowed by tiers of stacked, bald and battered retreads that Jessup had to slip through it sideways.

The manager of the place rushed up to them, rubbing his hands together in his eagerness to provide service. He took one look at all the guns and his big smile vanished. Jessup caught a glimpse of his back as he raced for the rear of the store, shouting and waving his arms. There was a sudden, brief commotion, the sound of breaking glass as manager and employees created their own emergency exit.

"Let's get on with it," Leon said, giving the fat Texan a shove in the direction the manager had gone.

The rear of the place was even more dismal than the front. Its crudely plastered walls were splattered with mud from the puddles on the dirt floor. There were tires and pieces of tires strewn in piles at odd intervals. Decorating the walls were rows of rusty wheels hanging from nails. The room's only window was crashed out; the employees had rammed an empty fifty-five-gallon oil drum through it to make their escape.

Leon patted Jessup down while his comrades kept gun muzzles tight to their captive's head. He fished the bulldog out of its ankle holder. "Hey, nice little piece," he said, hefting it appreciatively. He swung out the cylinder, spun it, then snapped it closed. He put it in his jacket pocket. "Thanks for the present. I may even kill you with it. But first..."

He picked a ball of heavy twine from the dirt and tossed it to one of the other men. "Tie him up real good and sit his big ass over on that pile of tires."

The man worked quickly, cinching Jessup's wrists together behind his back, then joining his ankles. Three of them shoved Jessup over onto the heap of scrap rubber.

"For the sake of our fallen buddies, we got to do something memorable to you," Leon told him.

He walked over to the room's only piece of modern equipment, an air compressor. He unscrewed the cap on the scarred gas tank and stuck in a finger. It came out wet. "Show time," he said, grabbing the starter rope and giving it a hard yank. The little two-stroke caught, chugging spastically. Leon found the throttle adjustment and evened out the idle. The red rubber compressor hose on the floor gave a sudden jerk and the nozzle end of it began to hiss.

Jessup watched Leon pick it up and squeeze the release valve lever. A gust of air blasted out. Leon aimed the nozzle at his own bare forearm and squeezed again. The jet of air pushed a deep dent into the muscle. Jessup didn't know what the bastard had in mind, but his intuition told him that whatever it was, he wasn't going to like it one bit.

"What do you say," Leon asked his men, "should we give Porky Pig a blow job?"

"A what?" one of the guys said doubtfully.

"Just hold his head, moron," Leon said. "I'll show you what I mean."

Jessup twisted away when they tried to grab him, shifting the point of his chin, trying to roll off the tires. He couldn't go anywhere. His rear end was through in the hole in the middle of the topmost tire and also through the holes in the next four, his knees elevated over his head. Still, it took three of them to pin his head down.

"Now, squeeze off his nose," Leon said.

One of the men caught Jessup's nose between thumb and forefinger, squashing it shut.

Leon shoved the air hose nozzle into the fat man's face, jamming it between his lips, against the front of his tightly clenched teeth. "Open wide," Leon said.

Jessup glared at him and kept his mouth shut.

"Okay, have it your way," Leon said, shoving the nozzle in the fat man's ear and squeezing the valve release.

Suddenly keeping his mouth shut wasn't so important to Jessup. The surge of air slammed into his ear drum like it was something solid, something long and thin and needle sharp. The pain was so unexpectedly intense, so overwhelming that it made him scream out loud.

Leon quickly switched orifices, ramming the brass fitting between Jessup's parted teeth, slipping the fingers of his free hand around the hose, clamping them over Jessup's mouth to form a tight seal.

Jessup gagged. The fitting tasted of old rubber and grit and gasoline. He thought he could keep the compressed air from reaching his lungs by constricting the muscles of his throat, closing off the passage. The second Leon opened the valve, he knew he was wrong. The force of the air was so strong that it seemed to swell his entire head. It ballooned his cheeks, bulged his eyes, blasted up into his sinuses. The only exit for the terrible pressure was his tear ducts; those tiny apertures spit both air and tears. And then he couldn't hold it off any longer. Air surged past the back of his tongue, rushed in a torrent down his throat. The sensation of being filled up against his will was as horrible as it was painful. Everything inside his chest, lungs, heart, bronchia, was expanding to the splitting point. For all the air he was getting, he could not breathe, air was drowning him.

"How many pounds per square inch will he take before he pops?" Leon asked the others as the compressor pumped on. He was having a high old time.

Walker Jessup, on the other hand, was dying.

O'TOOLE BARGED INTO the tourist souvenir shop and started yanking things off the wall.

The owner of the store, a small, very black man in a caftan and knit skullcap, watched in slack-jawed astonishment as the Westerner toppled the stunning warthog display, full-head mounts, mounted tusks, in his haste to get at the "authentic" tribal memorabilia.

Liam snatched a metal short sword from its wooden scabbard. He tested the edge with a thumb, then brought the blade slashing down on the nearest warthog head. The blade shattered like it was made of glass. He hurled the useless handle and cross guard against the far wall.

"Oh!" the shopkeeper said. "Oh, no! Stop!"

O'Toole tried another sword, with the same result. "Junk!" he raged, lunging for a zebra-skin covered shield and pair of crossed, wooden-shafted spears.

The shop owner likewise lunged for the red-haired man as he stabbed a spear at yet another expensive mounted head. The spear point, a triangular-shaped, double-edged blade, looked crusty and old but it was made of modern steel. It had been buried for six months to give it "antique" value. The long point penetrated the heavy pig skull to a depth of two and a half inches before it snapped off.

"What are you doing?" the merchant moaned, hanging onto O'Toole's brawny arm. "You're crazy! You're destroying my inventory!"

Liam shrugged the man off, thrust his hand in his pocket and came out with a fistful of money. He pushed it all into the shopkeeper's face. Then he grabbed two more spears off the wall and ran out of the store.

On the street, the locals knocked each other down trying to get out of the way of the furious-looking guy in white pants and a Hawaiian shirt, a spear-wielding holidaymaker.

Liam slowed as he neared the doorway Heiss's men had forced Jessup through. He crouched low and slipped soundlessly into the tire-repair shop. The service area was empty, but Liam heard noise coming from the back room. The drone of a small horsepower motor, the sound of whistling air and agonized whimpering. There were also occasional grunts of effort as if a prolonged struggle was in progress. He approached the open doorway leading to he next room with caution, keeping very low.

He stopped short. He could see the four mercs tussling with Jessup who was bound hand and foot and sitting on some old tires. Three of Heiss's men were trying to hold him down while the fourth held the end of a compressor hose stuffed in his mouth. The fat man's face was bloated, purpling under the grip of all those hands. Then one of the mercs said something, inaudible to O'Toole. It must have been cute, though, because the others all laughed.

Liam took it as his cue.

He sprang from his crouch, rushing them, the spear in his right hand cocked back. One of the men holding Jessup's head saw Liam coming and jerked upright, his mouth opening to cry a warning. With four powerful strides O'Toole built momentum, then, every ounce of his stocky body behind the throw, he let fly the spear, grunting with effort. Distance to target was less than twenty feet. Liam followed through, as if chucking the spear at a target thirty feet farther on. He followed through and kept on running, bringing up the second spear.

The point slammed into the standing man's center chest. The crude wooden shaft followed, burrowing in the slit the spearhead opened for it. The merc groaned and staggered back bug-eyed, against the piled tires, gripping the shaft with both hands, tugging at it futilely as his heart rattled to a stop.

The sight of their buddy suddenly impaled, froze the other mercs in place. O'Toole charged right into their midst, using the second spear like a lance. He drove it into the belly of a man on his left, then drove the man back into the wall, stabbing the spear point completely through him and deep into the plaster. Liam then threw his body against the side of the shaft, snapping the head off in the wall. With a savage twist, he ripped the shaft free of the man's stomach. As the fellow collapsed, slipping down the wall, blood and guts geysered from the terrible black vent below his navel.

"Kill him! Jesus, kill him!" Leon shouted reaching for the taped grip of the .45 auto tucked inside his belt.

O'Toole swiveled and sidekicked at the man's midline. The hard outside edge of his foot connected solidly with Leon's stomach.

The result was deafening.

The heavy caliber Colt, cocked, unlocked, its grip safety disconnected, discharged on impact inside the front of Leon's pants. The merc's eyes squashed shut, face screwed up tight as his knees buckled. He made no sound. There was nothing to say. Leon had given himself a brand-new asshole.

The surviving merc got his own pistol up and started shooting wildly at Liam, shooting as fast as he could pull the trigger. A 9 mm hollowpoint grazed the SOB's neck as he closed ground and swung the spear shaft like a baseball bat. It thwacked the merc across the bridge of the nose. The shock wave of impact rippled all the way to O'Toole's shoulders.

The merc stumbled backward, his high capacity 9 mm autoloader pointed at the ceiling, barking, belching yellow flame at the ceiling.

Liam, blood pouring down inside the collar of his shirt, knelt and retrieved Jessup's bulldog .44 which had fallen from Leon's pocket into the dirt. From a squatting position he shot the man once, double action in the head.

His ears ringing, O'Toole untied Jessup and after a couple of false starts helped him to his feet.

The fat Texan wiped his tongue on his necktie, regarding Liam with something akin to awe.

"You okay?"

"I take it all back," Jessup muttered.

"Take what back?" the red-haired man asked.

Jessup frowned as he surveyed O'Toole's violent handiwork. How did you tell a guy who just saved your ass that up until two minutes ago you considered him a no good drunk and a born loser? The answer was: you couldn't.

"Never mind," the fat man said. "Let's get the hell out of here."

10

As a precaution against their having been followed, Jessup made the taxi let them off a block from their destination, the warehouse where the arms were stored. Jessup paid the driver, then led O'Toole the long way around, down shambling packed-dirt lanes, between rows of wall-to-wall shanty houses that glowed soft yellow lantern light through curtainless, glassless windows. People who had nothing to hide. When he was certain there was no tail, Jessup took the red-haired man to the rendezvous point.

The narrow, two-story warehouse was built of red brick, pre-World War II; there were heavy iron bars on the tightly shuttered windows facing the street. There were no windows on the sides of the building. The double front doors were massive wooden structures reinforced with crude iron ribs. Jessup tried the single blackened knob, found the door bolted, then used a key on the lock. The place was dark when they entered. He said, "I guess the others haven't got here, yet."

"Guess again," a voice from the blackness answered.

When the lights came on, Jessup and O'Toole found themselves surrounded by armed SOBs.

"I see you located the weapons without any trouble," Jessup said.

"Machine tools," Barrabas said, lowering his heavy-barreled FN FAL. He scowled at O'Toole. The front of the Irish-American's aloha shirt was soaked through with blood. "What the hell happened to you?" he demanded. Then he said, "Better have a look, doc."

Lee Hatton was already on her way. She put her H&K submachine gun down on a crate lid and examined O'Toole's wound, turning his neck to the light. "That's a bullet track!"

O'Toole smiled sheepishly.

"This wildass saved my life," Jessup said. "With a pair of five dollar spears!"

"Is he okay?" Barrabas asked the medic.

"The bleeding's already stopped. An inch to the right and his heart would've pumped itself dry."

"Heiss?" the white-haired man said.

Jessup nodded. "There are four less of his mercs to deal with. That's the good news."

"And the bad?"

"We've got to move on them now, ASAP," Jessup said. "When Heiss's hit squad doesn't return on time, he's going to know something has gone seriously wrong. He's going to roll with the loot. The money could be on its way out the gate this very minute."

"Finish checking your weapons," Barrabas told his soldiers, then he saw to his own gun. He removed the loaded 20-round box mag from the FN FAL and pulled back the bolt, checking the chamber and feedway. After making sure the weapon was unloaded he let the bolt slide forward. He released the horizontal catch at the rear left of the receiver and broke open the hinged action. He drew the bolt cover off the receiver, removed the bolt assembly by pulling on the return spring rod. He looked down the gleaming bore. Satisfied, he quickly reassembled the FAL. It was a heavy weapon, more than thirteen pounds. A bonafide machine rifle, it would handle light MG duties nicely. Barrabas folded up the bipod, put the buttstock on the floor and leaned the FAL against the inside of his knee.

The fat man winked at him, then picked up a crowbar, walked over to an unopened crate and proceeded to pry the lid off. From the excelsior packing, he took a padded black garment. He tossed it over to Nanos.

"Now you're talking!" the Greek said, undoing the Velcro fasteners and shrugging into the body armor.

"Class IV," Jessup said, passing out vests to the others. "They'll stop .223 and .308 hard-core ammo."

"Hey, where's yours?" Nanos asked the fat man. Jessup shrugged. "I got a charmed life."

"What he means," O'Toole told Lee as she finished bandaging up his neck wound, "is that they don't make 'em that big."

The doctor shook her head. "What he means," she said, "is that as usual he'll be bringing up the rear."

"Don't forget the war paint," Billy Two said, passing out flat tins of camo.

The SOBs and Jessup began to smear their hands and faces with black grease. All except Hayes. He just sat back and laughed.

"What's so funny?" Billy Two said.

"You are the sorriest looking minstrel show I have ever seen."

Barrabas tossed a can of makeup into Hayes's lap. "You, too, Claude," he said. "If light hits the oil on your skin you could get us all killed."

"Yeah, I know," Hayes said, slapping the grease on his cheeks. "I was only kidding."

"And you, Liam, get out of those goddamn white pants."

"Yes, Colonel." O'Toole accepted the pair of dark khaki fatigues that Nanos thrust at him.

Jessup then passed out pairs of black leather gloves to everyone. "You'll need these to get over the perimeter wall," he explained. "They've topped it with slivers of glass."

When everyone was ready to roll, Barrabas ran through the script one last time, spreading out the sketch of the Crusade '85 mansion on the lid of a crate. He pointed at the small gate house adjacent and inside the large front gateway. "The key is getting control of the gate," he said. "If we can't open it, we can't get the money out."

"The doc and I will handle it," O'Toole said.

Barrabas looked at Nanos and Billy Two.

The Indian answered the unasked question. "We cut off the main building from the parking apron, so you and Hayes can hot-wire the truck."

"The money had better be in it," Barrabas told the fat man. "We aren't going to have time to go rooting through sacks of grain to make sure."

"I watched them pack the truck yesterday. The money's in there, all right."

"No last-minute questions?" Barrabas asked, looking from SOB to SOB. "Problems?"

Nobody said a word.

"Then, let's hit it."

Jessup led them out the warehouse's rear entrance and over to a 6x6 truck parked under a rickety shed. O'Toole got behind the wheel and the fat man rode shotgun. The rest of the SOBs piled into the covered bed, pulled up and locked the tailgate.

Nanos reached out and touched the olive drab, Conestoga-style top. He made a face in the darkness. "This canvas crap sure as hell isn't going to slow down the incoming."

It was something none of them needed to be reminded about as the truck rumbled to life.

Nanos mistook silence for interest. He went on, "You'd think Shamu could've at least gotten us one of those armor-plated Commie 6x6s. What do you call 'em? BTR 152s? The ones with firing ports on both..."

Barrabas's disembodied voice cut him off. "Alex, shut the fuck up."

11

Dr. Tuttle Lalarva stood on the balcony of his suite, which overlooked the rear of the mansion's grounds. He stared across the back gardens at the tall stand of eucalyptus, floodlit from below by the security klieg lights. Beyond the trees was a solid twelve-foot-high wall. He had come to hate the sight of that perimeter wall. He hated it because it didn't keep Ethiopia out. Even a two-hundred-foot-high wall could not have insulated him from the sounds of the place or the smell of its people. What he required and could not have was a hermetically sealed dome with a self-contained air and water supply. A dome of opaque glass that blotted out the very existence of what he deemed a "Third World sewer." As much as he loathed the country and people he exploited, on the eve of his departure Dr. Lalarva loathed leaving them even more.

Tonight he was stepping off the end of the earth. Trading known perils for the unknown. He had no choice. Among the known perils was swift, certain death at the hands of his business partner, Karl Heiss.

From the start of their association, their very first meeting under the aegis of the CIA, Heiss had scared the hell out of Lalarva. There was something inhuman about him, a kind of coldness he radiated even when he was laughing at one of his own jokes. It wasn't the calculating coldness he had seen in some other men, the power to block normal feelings; Heiss possessed no normal human feelings. The cold he gave off was alien, as if inside his head the brain of a highly evolved insect operated his human limbs. Lalarva had looked into Heiss's eyes four months ago and seen the voracious cockroach lurking there behind them. He had known at once he was marked for death. There was too much money involved. Heiss would not share it when he could have it all.

Tonight the time had come for Lalarva to cut and run. To salvage what he could of his operation, what the Dergue would let him have. Out of the thirty million in cash, he would get five million for himself. It was enough to start a new life, if need be. It was also enough to forge on with the old one. If half the world branded him a thief, the other half would surely hold him up as a saint. With the right legal team behind him he could stonewall his way through a decade of Federal Grand Jury hearings while he returned in triumph and white satin robes to his beloved San Fernando Valley, its malls, its shopping centers, its freeways. Karl Heiss was all that stood in his way.

More important by far than the cash in hand, the Dergue had allowed Lalarva to make his scheduled live satellite plea for funds. Asrat and his uneducated cronies had no idea how much such a broadcast could be worth when milked by a professional machine. The contributions often came in too fast to be counted. But not too fast to be dumped wholesale into a funnel of complex international accounts. The small end of the vast Crusade '85 funnel was situated in Lalarva's back pocket. Three weeks after the broadcast, he expected to have fully recouped his losses to the Dergue.

The satellite fund-raiser would be the crowning moment of Lalarva's cable video career. The ultimate huckster making the most heart-rending and widely viewed appeal for mass salvation in the history of the world.

And what of the refugees, in whose name he begged, pleaded, sobbed? In the grand order of things, San Fernando Valley style, of what importance were they, really? Would they ever buy a stereo on time? A refrigerator-freezer? Would they ever hold a major credit card? If they did not consume, then they would be consumed. It was a law of nature. Their only importance was to serve as bait.

Their expressions of agony stimulated a knee-jerk response, the blind giving of money.

Though Lalarva had bought his Ph.D. in Sociology mail order, for less than one hundred dollars, he was not completely ignorant of the lessons of history. He had styled his "Crusade '85" after the Holy Crusades of the Middle Ages. It was an excuse to pillage and plunder in the name of piety.

There was still the matter of Heiss.

Lalarva turned on the balcony, putting the trees and the wall behind him. He walked back through the double French doors to his bedroom. His small suitcase lay packed but still open on the bed. He stepped to the bureau and opened the bottom drawer, pulling it all the way out, setting it on its nose so he could get at the back. Taped to the outside of the drawer's back was a small, stainless-steel automatic pistol. He pulled the gun free, then stripped off the tape that still stuck to it.

The AMT backup fit easily inside his cupped hand. He ejected the five-shot magazine and looked at the hollowpoint .380 caliber bullets. The little pistol was meant to perform up close, virtually point blank. That fit Lalarva as well because he was no crack shot. In fact, he had never fired a weapon in anger before. He had practiced with the little gun in secret for months, palming it, swinging it up and firing all five as fast as he could squeeze the trigger at a head-sized target. After going through several hundred rounds of ammunition he had gotten his killing range inside three feet.

Which left him plenty of margin for error, as he intended to put the muzzle to Heiss's temple the moment Asrat's forces halted the money convoy.

He reinserted the magazine, chambered a round and slipped the gun into the outside right-hand pocket of his sport jacket. His palms were all sweaty. He wiped them off on his handkerchief. He did not look forward to killing the man face-to-face, but it was infinitely preferable to being killed by him.

A knock on his bedroom door made him jerk and jam his hand down into his pocket, down over the tiny gun. "What do you want?" he asked, his heart thumping.

"Heiss says it's time to go."

It was one of the mercenaries.

"I won't be a minute," Lalarva told him. He closed his suitcase and sat down on the edge of the bed. One last time, he told himself, drawing a calming breath. Run through it one last time.

He turned to his left and said aloud, "What are they stopping for?" As he spoke, his right hand dipped into his jacket pocket and came up with the AMT. His thumb touched the manual safety but this time did not actually disengage it. In one motion, he raised the gun to shoulder height and shoved it across the gap between the imaginary car's front seats. Muzzle to the driver's temple, he squeezed.

And squeezed.

And squeezed.

12

As the SOBs crossed the last intersection between themselves and the Crusade '85 mansion, Nile Barrabas rapped his knuckles on the grimy window between truck bed and cab. "Cut the lights," he said through the glass, raising his voice so it was audible over the considerable hum of a half dozen heavy-duty tires on asphalt.

O'Toole obeyed, slapping the switch on the dashboard. The road ahead went dark. The 6x6 followed the curve of the street to the right. Even though it was a very high-class neighborhood there were no streetlights. The row of mansions were all shielded from the street by high walls and set apart from each other by open ground. The street itself ended in a cul-de-sac.

As O'Toole drove past their intended target, Barrabas pulled aside a corner of the Conestoga. The front of the grounds, the heavy gate, wall and street were floodlit. The gate was solid metal and moved on a narrow track set in the paving. It was motor driven. Over the top of the gate he could see the roofline and third story of the Georgian-style mansion. Nothing else was visible.

O'Toole drove the truck to the end of the street, then parked it facing the way they had come, so that the mansion gate was visible to the driver. He left the engine running and climbed down from the cab. As he did so, Jessup climbed over the gearshift lever and slid behind the steering wheel.

The rest of the SOBs quickly joined O'Toole on the road.

Barrabas addressed the fat man up in the truck cab. "Don't take your eyes off the front of the place. At the first sign of trouble, this junker better be rolling, on its way to pick us up and get us the hell out."

"Not to worry," Jessup said, taking out his heavy revolver and putting it up on the dash within easy reach. "I won't let you down."

"Okay, let's move," the white-haired man said, unshouldering his FN FAL from its sling, holding it by the folding handle placed forward and above the magazine housing at the weapon's precise center of gravity.

They kept to the deep shadows of scrub, sliding along in a ragged but silent skirmish line. Within fifty feet of the wall the security lights eliminated all shadow. They formed a bright halo that made everything visible in stark, contrasting shades of black and gray. There were no guard towers or gun turrets along the top of the wall, perhaps the architect could find no way to tastefully render them? If there were guns trained on the illuminated no-man's land, they were stationed out of sight on the upper floor or roof of the mansion.

Barrabas had no intention of standing there in the hard glare to find out. He took the lead, waving his soldiers on. He watched the roofline as he charged the wall, watched for muzzle flash. As he neared the barrier, it switched allegiances, became his defense, the top of the wall shielding him from the upper story of the house. Two more long strides and he was there. He put his back to the wall. O'Toole, Hatton, Hayes, Starfoot and Nanos moved in on either side of him. Despite the light, he couldn't clearly make out the features of their faces. Thanks to the black camo, he could only see their eyes. They were as big and bright as hen's eggs, pumped with adrenaline. Barrabas, too, felt the familiar rush, the sense of impending cataclysm. In a single instant, over the pounding of his heart, the rasp of his breathing, he heard the sound of crickets, an airplane passing to the east, a twig snapping under O'Toole's boot; he smelled wood smoke and jasmine; he felt the reassuring weight of the machine rifle in his hand. He smiled, his teeth very white against the dead black of his face. Then he nodded to the others.

Billy Two gave him a nonregulation salute and he and Nanos took off along the wall toward the back of the mansion.

Barrabas waited a beat, giving them time to log some distance, then he and Hayes followed. They ran beside the wall, heading away from the street, and made position just after Billy Two and Nanos reached theirs.

At the same moment, the three teams, O'Toole and Lee, Barrabas and Hayes, Billy Two and Nanos, shouldered their weapons and scaled the wall at the prearranged points.

As the fat man had warned, the top of the foot-and-a-half-thick wall was decorated with wicked upraised spikes of broken glass. They had been set right in the mortar. Barrabas used gloved hands to pick his way up and over the glittering obstacle course. He dropped soundlessly to the other side, landing in a soft cushion of wet eucalyptus leaves.

There was a terrible drought in the rest of the country, but the carefully manicured gardens and lawns of the Crusade '85 estate hadn't suffered from it. Everything glistened with moisture from a recent and copious sprinkling.

Barrabas unslung the heavy-barreled FAL and knelt behind a tree trunk that blocked him from mansion's view. As he did so, he thumbed the fire-selector switch, on left side of the grip, all the way down. Full-auto. He shouldered the weapon and, bracing it against the side of the tree, swung its sights over the parking apron, front and side of the house.

There was no movement in that direction.

Hayes dropped from the wall, landing behind him. The black man came up with the silenced muzzle of the MP5 SD3 out in front, ready to rip.

They listened for a moment from the cover of the tree.

The only loud sounds came from outside the estate. Isolated traffic. Dogs barking a long way off.

Barrabas slipped out from behind the tree and ran straight and low across the lawn to the shrubs that bordered the brick parking apron. He dropped to his belly behind one, quickly unfolded the FAL's bipod and set up shop from a rock-steady three-point stance. Hayes split off to the right and took position behind a similar screen of juniper.

Again Barrabas listened, straining. Again he heard nothing inside the compound. Any second now, he thought, and the gate house would fall. He could not wait longer.

Ahead of him, three cars and a heavy truck were parked in front of the mansion's broad stairs. The bright light from the house reflected the two BMWs and the Mercedes on the apron's wet bricks. A 6x6 stood across from them, on the other side of the mansion entrance.

Barrabas jumped up and ran. The nearest car was seventy-five feet away, across the flat, deadly expanse of the parking area. If he was going to draw fire from the house, he was going to draw it now. He could hear Hayes's footfalls behind him. They both reached the side of the BMW at the same moment, Hayes ducking down next to the front wheels, Barrabas the back. He peered around the BMW's rear end.

No sentry.

No dogs.

Nothing.

Barrabas frowned. He found it hard to believe that they had really caught Heiss napping. But if they had, Barrabas was going to make damn sure he never woke up.

Cautiously, the white-haired man rounded the rear of the car in a crouch, picking up speed as he moved for the next vehicle, about twenty feet away. He was four feet from the back wheels of the BMW when his luck abruptly turned.

One second the way was clear, the next, he was staring across the BMW's trunk lid, face-to-face with a very startled sentry. The man was wearing external body armor, just like Barrabas and he had an Uzi SMG in his hands.

The guy was startled, but definitely a pro. He recovered the same instant Barrabas did. They both brought their guns around. The sentry had a slight advantage because his weapon was shorter, pointed quicker.

Before Barrabas could get on track, he was tracked. The quick burst of autofire caught him full in the chest, driving him back a step. He returned fire off balance, by reflex, holding the heavy rifle one-handed, the pain of bullet impacts causing him to deathgrip and pin the trigger.

A flurry of 7.62 mm slugs slammed into the merc's center chest. Unlike the 9 mm rounds that hit Barrabas and were stopped, trapped by his body armor, the heavier, much faster NATO AP slugs punched through ballistic nylon like it was a cotton/polyester blend. Blood spurted from the holes in the front of the man's vest, splashing the BMW's rear deck lid. He clutched his chest and toppled to his back.

The answering fire from the mansion's entryway came almost at once. It was both accurate and heavy. Barrabas dove for cover behind the rear wheels as a volley of slugs shattered in the side windows and slammed the car's body, rattling it on its springs like a tree caught in a high wind from hell.

DR. LEE HATTON and Liam O'Toole dropped over the wall and followed it along the mansion's front border until they had their target in sight.

The gate house was actually a small cottage and stood in a bright pool of light at the edge of the parking apron.

O'Toole nudged the doctor and they crept closer.

The place had windows on all sides. The windows were open, but screened against insects. Through the screens O'Toole and Lee could see two men seated at a small desk.

As they watched, one of the men stood up and, with his back angled toward them, stretched. He was armed. A high-capacity auto pistol in a shoulder rig.

"How're we going to do this?" Lee asked in a whisper.

"I'll take the window facing the house. You take the one on this side. We count to ten, then pop up and shoot 'em through the screens."

"Sounds okay to me," she said, grinning. "I know how to count to ten."

They crawled the last twenty-five feet, right up to the cottage. Then O'Toole gave her the "go" sign and moved out of sight, around the side of the little building. In her head, the doctor began the count, "One thousand one, one thousand two..." She rose to her feet, straightened up, and put her back to the gate-house wall. When she reached the number "nine," she gripped the German SMG in both hands, bracing its retractable butt stock against her hip. On the count of "ten" she swung around and stepped in front of the window.

Right away she knew she'd messed up. In her excitement, she'd counted too fast.

O'Toole was nowhere to be seen.

The two mercs were frozen in time.

One of them faced her, the one still seated. He had his hands behind his head, his feet up on the desk. He had on a body-armor vest. It was getting to be quite the rage in certain circles. She could see the scuffed soles of his shoes. Then he saw her as well. Muttering a curse, he lunged for the Uzi that lay in the middle of the desktop.

The other man, also in armor, had his back turned to her. At the warning from his friend, he reached for his pistol, pivoting, dropping to one knee as the weapon cleared leather and came around.

Then the scene disintegrated.

Lee was unsure if she or Liam started shooting first. Not that it mattered in the least. The two-man cross fire they orchestrated was perfectly withering. From opposing ninety-degree positions, they both swept the tiny room with a hail of silenced autofire. The seated sentry took multiple hits in the head and chest. Only the head hits counted. And there were plenty of them. They were all through and through, slugs and cranial contents smacking the wall behind. She saw the soles of the man's shoes one more time as both he and his chair fell over backward in a tangled heap.

The standing man did not stand for long.

He got his handgun up and pointed at O'Toole, but never fired a shot. Lee swung up and through her target, trigger pinned back, SMG chugging. His unprotected armpit, exposed by the Weaver stance he had assumed, soaked up half a clip of 9 mm parabellums. These, however, did not go through and through. There were too many vital organs to slow them down. The merc crumpled, twisting from the impacts. He was dead before his butt hit the floor.

Only when it was over, when the shredded screens stopped trembling, did the doctor allow herself to hear the noise of battle still ringing in her head. There was noise, too. The muzzle blasts had been silenced but the hits had not. They sounded like a pool cue smacking into a hundred pounds of hamburger. Over and over. She smelled cordite, saw clouds of it sweep past the lights, watched it still curl from the fat muzzle and the ejection port of her submachine gun.

Lee Hatton shivered, sealing it all out. She cracked in a fresh mag and joined Liam at the gatehouse door. He opened it and they entered, quickly checking the corpses on the floor.

"This must be the switch," O'Toole said, straightening up, pointing at a lever beside the door.

It only had two positions, forward and back. It was forward now and the gate was closed.

"Pull it back," the doctor said.

Just as she spoke, gunfire erupted from the direction of the mansion and the money truck.

O'Toole's hand stopped in midair.

"Damn!" he said. "We're going to have to fight our way out."

The firing suddenly intensified and stray bullets from across the apron thudded into the outside of the gate house, forcing them to duck down.

Then the lever controlling the gate jerked back.

"No!" Lee said as the gate motor whirred. "Don't open it! Not till we've got control of the goods!"

"Dammit, I didn't open it!" O'Toole protested. He grabbed the lever and tried to force it back. He could not.

The front gate slowly, smoothly began to roll back.

From the parking apron, headlights flared, engines roared amid the gunshots.

Lee knew exactly what was happening.

It was all coming apart.

13

Karl Heiss glared at his wristwatch. I'll give him another minute, he thought, and then I'm going up there myself and drag the yellow bastard down by the back of his collar.

No sooner had he thought it, than Dr. Tuttle Lalarva descended the spiral staircase, valise in hand.

"So glad you could join us," Heiss said, coldly. If the man hadn't been an indispensible part of Heiss's plan to reach the Sudanese border, he would've gladly left him behind. With a bullet in his head.

The eleven mercenaries in his employ shifted about the foyer anxiously. They, like Heiss, were eager to be off.

"Sorry," Lalarva said, meekly. As he reached the foot of the stairs he asked, "Did the four you sent out to take care of Jessup come back, yet?"

"No," Heiss answered curtly. "Something obviously has gone wrong. Again."

"But Jessup was alone," Lalarva said.

"Leon and the others have done something stupid. Either they're dead or they've been captured by the police. We can't wait here any longer."

The surviving mercenaries nodded to each other. Waiting in the wrong place could get you killed.

"If everything's loaded, let's go," Heiss said, gesturing for the group to make a mass exit.

As the first merc reached the door, automatic weapon fire shattered the night's calm.

"Jesus, we're bein' hit!" one of the soldiers for hire cried. "They're in the damn compound!"

Karl Heiss reacted instantly, following a much-rehearsed script of his own devising. "Hit them back!" he shouted, shoving the mercs nearest him toward the door. To the petrified Lalarva he yelled, "Open the gate switch!" The order shocked the con man out of his panic trance. As Lalarva operated the lever that overrode the gate-house control of the motorized barrier, the mercenaries rushed out the front door, shooting at the intruders. Before joining them, Heiss yanked the switch that opened the mansion's kennels, releasing the pack of dogs onto the grounds.

The mercenaries had taken positions behind a pair of huge stone lions that flanked the entry stairs. Heiss ducked and sprinted through the clouds of gunsmoke, dropping behind the closest lion.

"Where are they?" he demanded over the din of full-auto fusilade.

The man next to him pointed. "One of them's behind the brown BMW."

As Heiss looked at the indicated spot, a head popped up around the car's back bumper, orange light flickered at him. A hail of bullets swept the house front, sang off the stone lion's back, marble sparking blue and hot.

Heiss flattened, frantically brushing the molten bits off his hair. The head behind the car. He had only seen it for a second, but the afterimage had burned into his retina. He was sure the hair on that head had been white. His heart thudded up in his throat. It couldn't be, he told himself. Nile Barrabas, his hated enemy, was dead, killed along with his SOBs by crack units of Soviet Military Intelligence. Heiss felt fear suddenly clutch at his bowels. What if Barrabas wasn't dead? What if the white-haired man was still alive, working for Walker Jessup or the CIA? Alive and about to finally take his long-overdue vengeance? "Pour it on him!" Heiss shouted at the top of his lungs.

The mercenaries sent a wall of lead at the BMW. Heiss watched from behind one of the stone lion's forepaws as all four tires exploded and the car dropped abruptly onto its rims. Glass from the shattering front windshield sprayed the bricks, and the rear trunk lid sprang up of its own volition.

Then the man behind the car took off. He ran like a madman, juking across the apron, away from the house.

His hair was stark white.

"Kill him! Kill him! Goddamn you!" Heiss shrieked.

The mercenaries tracked the fleeing figure with their SMGs, bullets skipping off the bricks. He vaulted a shrub and shot across the broad lawn.

They had him.

They had him cold.

Slugs from the direction of the gate house raked Heiss's position, forcing the mercenaries to stop firing and take cover. Heiss watched in slack-jawed horror as the white-haired man escaped to the tree line, unscathed.

There was no time to consider the implications. The gate was fully open.

"Come on! Everybody!" Heiss yelled. "Everybody out!"

The mercenaries broke from cover and ran for the money truck. Heiss and Lalarva raced for the turbo-charged Mercedes four-door sedan. As Heiss jerked open the driver's door, slugs plowed into it. He dove across the front seats and jammed the key in the ignition. Lalarva piled into the back, throwing himself to the floor behind the front seat.

Heiss started up the Mercedes at the same moment the money truck lurched forward, roaring for the gate. He put the car in gear and, his body still across the front seats, popped the clutch. Drive wheels spinning, he swerved the Mercedes to the right, jamming his front bumper into the back of the money truck. He didn't dare rise up to check his angle at the gate. He was making a daisy chain, betting that the driver of the truck knew where he was going. As Heiss passed by the gate house, the car's driver-side windows imploded, showering him with shards of glass.

Then they were out on the street.

Heiss pushed up, wrenching the steering wheel hard over as the Mercedes jumped the opposite curb. He pushed his foot down hard on the gas, powering his way out of the sickening slide. The car jolted as it hopped back onto the pavement, its turbo-charger whining. Heiss had to hit the brakes to keep from crashing into the rear of the 6x6.

One of the mercs in the bed of the money truck waved back at him and gave a thumbs-up sign.

Everything was okay.

He looked in his rearview mirror for Lalarva. The man was nowhere in sight. "Hey, we're in the clear, now," he said.

No reply.

"Did you faint or just wet your pants?"

In the rearview mirror Heiss saw Lalarva raise his head above the top of the seat. His face was green.

"A little of both, huh?" Heiss said.

14

"Here, Alex," Billy Two hissed over his shoulder.

"Ouch!"

"What?" the Indian said, turning. "Alex, are you okay?"

"Lousy sprinkler head," Nanos muttered, kneeling down.

"I thought it was something serious."

"Stubbed hell out of my toe."

"Should I call an ambulance?"

"Hey, I'm really hurting."

"In that case I think we'd better get your mom."

"Think again, you asshole," Nanos snapped back, straightening. He took a couple of tentative, hobbling steps. "Holy shit," he groaned. "It feels like I ripped my whole frigging big toenail off."

Billy Two shook his head. "You're gonna have to guts up, man." As the Indian turned back toward the front corner of the mansion, a salvo of shots rang out.

The two big men flattened themselves against the wall of the house. One automatically covered their rear, the other took point. Gunfire raged from the front of the building. At least a dozen full-auto weapons were clattering away.

"Holy shit, those aren't our guns. We've got a goddamn war on our hands."

"Come on," the Indian said. "Let's go have us a look-see."

They edged forward, rounding the corner in time to see the whole Heiss team abandon their position on the front steps and dash for the vehicles on the parking apron.

"Dammit, the gate's opening!" Billy said, bringing up his heavy-barreled FN FAL. He had to do something. He fired from the hip, sending twenty armor-piercing rounds streaking across the apron at belly height. There were two BMWs blocking his line of fire. He shot all holy hell out of them. His human targets merely ducked down behind the disintegrating machines. When he came up empty, they continued on to the money truck and Mercedes.

"They're rolling!" Nanos shouted, stepping out as his friend jumped back to reload. He sprayed the rear end of the fishtailing Mercedes with 9 mm lead. It kept right on going past the gate.

A man with white hair crossed the lawn about thirty yards from them, heading for the gate house.

"It's the colonel! Let's go!" Billy said.

He took off at top speed, leaving Nanos to hop as best he could on his own.

"Hey, wait!" Nanos called to the Indian's already distant back. "Wait, you bastard." He looked behind him. "I hear something," he said to himself, quickly stripping out his empty mag and cracking in a new one. "Sounds like..."

Around the back corner of the building fifteen or twenty mangy-looking dogs scrambled toward him. They ran in a pack, jaws open, howling. Watching them in the hard glow of the security lights he was reminded of Tiajuana, greyhounds at the night races barreling around the far turn.

And he was the poor little rabbit.

"Hold it, you suckers!" Nanos growled, shooting a 5-round burst over their heads. The silenced weapon had no deterrent effect. The dogs charged on.

A horn sounded behind him.

Jessup had pulled the 6x6 in front of the open gate. The other SOBs were piling in. Nanos turned and ran as if the hounds of hell were on his ass. Which they were. He forgot his ripped toenail. He forgot everything but keeping ahead of all those rows of teeth.

He hit the bricks of the parking apron high-kicking. He could hear doggy claws scrabbling for traction behind him.

Come on, come on, he told himself as the pack cut the distance between them to ten feet.

Maybe it was even closer than that.

As he flew out the gate toward the already rolling 6x6 he could see the faces of the SOBs in the truck bed. They looked worried.

"Jump for it!" Billy Two shouted, leaning over the tailgate and holding out his hand.

Nanos took a little staggerstep to time the leap and in so doing lost precious ground. As he jumped, something hit him squarely in the back. He caught Billy's hand and hung on as the truck picked up speed. Billy just stared at him as did the others. He made no attempt to lift him into the truck.

"Pull me up!"

"No way!" Billy said.

Then Nanos felt the shaking, heard the snarling. There was a goddam dog on his back! It had fastened its jaws in the Kevlar and was going crazy, trying to rip out a bite-sized chunk.

"Give the dog the jacket," Barrabas said, grabbing Nanos's other arm, pulling him up so his feet didn't drag along the ground.

Liam undid the Velcro closures and the weight dropped from the Greek's back.

As they pulled him in, Alex glanced at the road behind. The pack had closed in tight and was savagely attacking the discarded armor.

"You're lucky it didn't get hold of the seat of your pants," O'Toole said. "Or that would be your butt back there."

"It was almost all our butts," Barrabas said, grimly.

"We haven't lost yet, Colonel," Lee said. "They can't go any faster than we can."

Hayes turned back from the cab's rear window. "They've only got a three-minute lead."

"O'Toole," Barrabas said, "you get up front and take over the driving. Pedal to the metal."

The stocky Irish-American nodded eagerly then crawled under the Conestoga cover, heading for the driver's side of the truck cab.

The truck swerved wildly as Jessup turned the controls over to O'Toole. Once he was behind the wheel it settled down. He threw a smooth-as-butter double-clutch, dropping the engine into a lower gear. Winding. Winding. Squeezing the absolute maximum acceleration out of the 6x6.

His upshift was just as clean.

It gave Barrabas cause for hope.

It made the other SOBs send up a cheer.

If they could only land a little bit of luck, they had one chance in hell.

Definitely their kind of odds.

15

Dr. Lalarva had not wet his pants.

But he was teetering on the verge.

The unexpected and brutal assault on the mansion, and their wild, almost suicidal escape had upset the alrcady delicate balance of his nerves. He looked at Karl Heiss in the rearview mirror, saw the man laughing at him, at his distress, and Lalarva's confusion and fear turned to shame.

Then shame turned to hate.

Heiss acted as if he, the Roach King, was the supreme judge of every other creature that drew breath. It was a ludicrous idea on its face. The man was a piece of scum, by any yardstick. It wouldn't have mattered in the least that he had judged Lalarva spineless and parasitical, if said judgment hadn't confirmed the man's own secret self-evaluation.

Lalarva plunged his hand into the side pocket of his sport coat. He was afraid, all right. And the feel of the AMT's grip hard against his palm did not reassure him. His mind reeled with the dire consequences that would result if, by chance, he happened to miss. Heiss would not laugh off a bungled attempt on his life. Heiss would kill him, for sure, but he would not give him a clean death. Dr. Lalarva visualized himself gutshot and dumped out of the car somewhere between Addis and Khartoum, left to fight off the buzzards until his strength was gone. Then they would land on his still-heaving chest, dig their talons into his flesh and fight over the prizes: his eyes, his tongue.

He caught himself up short. What was he worrying about? Circumstances had made the job even easier than originally planned. He was in the back seat, directly behind his intended target. His hands were out of sight. There was no danger of the gun getting hung up in his pocket on the quickdraw. He could put the pistol against the man's head and fire before Heiss knew what hit him. The back seat was better for regaining control of the car after the killing, too. Lalarva could reach over the corpse and steer with both hands.

Heiss's eyes flicked from the mirror, back to the street as he turned with the curve of the road, following the money truck dead ahead.

Lalarva knew Major General Asrat's ambush was set up at the first intersection, roughly forty yards away and closing. He carefully took the stainless-steel AMT out of his pocket, keeping his hand well down.

"There's no danger, now. Why don't you sit back and enjoy yourself?" Heiss said. "Unless you think you'd be more comfortable face down on the floor?"

Lalarva pretended to ignore the remark and continued to look straight ahead. He released the compact automatic's thumb safety and shifted the weapon around in his hand, making sure he had a firm hold on it. During practice his hand had a habit of necking up on the grip after the second shot in a rapid-fire sequence. He wanted to unload all five cartridges under complete control.

The money truck gained speed as it neared the intersection, pulling slightly away from the tailing Mercedes. Lalarva watched it carefully. He knew what was going to happen.

Everything started out according to plan. As the money truck approached the cross street, another truck, just as big, its front end sticking out into the intersection from the street on the left, suddenly lurched ahead, surging out into the middle of the road.

"Goddamn!" Heiss snarled as brake lights flashed in front of him and the money truck went into a skid.

Lalarva brought the gun up and held it on top of the seat, hidden by the back of his left hand.

There was supposed to be an accident. The ambush truck was supposed to completely block the intersection, forcing a collision, forcing the money truck to stop.

Instead, the ambush truck stopped.

Lalarva couldn't believe his eyes.

It stopped two-thirds of the way across the intersection, leaving a gap of eight or nine feet between its front bumper and the street corner.

The money truck cut hard over to the right, so hard that the wheels on that side all broke free of the asphalt. It jumped the curb and grazed the ambush vehicle, smashing its headlights and radiator. It smashed and kept on rolling, careering through the inersection. As it passed the ambush truck a volley of shots rang out.

Heiss slashed the Mercedes over as well, making the radials squeal, driving Lalarva headfirst into the rear door. The ambush truck was moving again, moving to close the gap as Heiss shot through it. Riflemen standing behind the truck opened fire as the Mercedes whipped by.

Ahead of them, the money truck narrowly missed hitting the building on the far right corner of the intersection. After rolling over thirty feet of sidewalk, it veered abruptly back onto the road.

Heiss followed the wild path of the money truck, cutting the wheel frantically back to the left, climbing the curb to avoid slamming head-on into the building on the far corner.

Lalarva had dropped his weapon on the carpeted floor. Clutching the seat back for all he was worth, he looked out the Mercedes's rear window.

Asrat had finally blocked the intersection with the truck, but too late.

They were past it.

"What the hell is going on?" Heiss said, scowling into the rearview mirror. His face seemed to have lost all of its smugness and much of its color. "You didn't see a white-haired man back at the mansion, did you? One of the bastards who attacked us?"

Heiss's tone of voice was strange. A little shrill. A little panicked. He went on talking without waiting for Lalarva's reply.

"This whole thing stinks of him! Jesus Christ, he could have a goddamn army lined up in front of us. We could be running right into his hands! I was stupid, *stupid* to believe he was really dead. To believe when I didn't see the son of a bitch's corpse with my own eyes. To believe when I didn't hack open his chest and cut out his dead heart with my own hands, crush it under my heel."

The tirade made no sense to Lalarva. He picked up his pistol from the floorboard.

Heiss slammed his hand down on top of the steering wheel, making the car do a gut-wrenching jitterstep. "Bastard!" he raged. "Barrabas, you bloody bastard!"

Lalarva had the gun in his hand and he didn't know what to do with it. If he shot Heiss now, he would lose the money truck. He would have nothing. Nothing but the pleasure of seeing the man's brains splattered over the dashboard, the pleasure of shutting him up once and for all.

Pleasure would have to wait.

Lalarva engaged the AMT's thumb safety and slipped the weapon back into his pocket, confident that he had made the right decision.

Heiss glared at him in the rearview and said, "What the hell are you grinning at?"

MAJOR GENERAL ASRAT had been assured by his subordinates, and Lt. Hailu in particular, that absolutely nothing could go wrong with the ambush. The blocking maneuver with the truck had been practiced several times during the course of the evening when there was no pedestrian or auto traffic to take notice. The platoon of handpicked soldiers had been kept carefully hidden behind the canvas flaps that covered the back of the truck. The ambush team had been drilled beforehand at another location, drilled with live ammunition. They knew their job.

When the gunfire from the mansion began, Asrat was sitting in the front seat of an unmarked sedan across the street from the ambush truck. As he listened to the unmistakable sounds of combat he felt a terrible sinking in his stomach. Something clearly had gone wrong. And before his operation had even begun.

Hailu, he fumed, bolting from the car and running across the deserted street. Where the hell was the man when he needed him? The lieutenant had disappeared over an hour ago and had not been seen since. Asrat ran to the rear of the parked truck and threw back one of the canvas flaps. "Out!" he said to the rows of men seated in darkness. "On the double!"

The troops poured from the truck carrying AK-47s with 30-round, curved magazines.

"Take position," Asrat said, waving his men to the side of the truck opposite the mansion.

The shooting from that direction swelled to a popping fury, then dwindled off. Whatever had happened, it was over. The major general took a wide stance near the nose of the truck, putting his hands on his hips as he surveyed the empty road. No change in plans was called for. The cul-de-sac was a peculiarity of terrain that worked in Asrat's favor no matter what. If some other group had tried to rob the Crusade and succeeded, or if Karl Heiss managed to keep the loot, the only route out was in the major general's control.

He heard the rumble of engines in the distance. Turning to the line of men beside the truck, he said, "Get ready. They're coming."

The bolts on thirty AKs clacked as his soldiers charged their weapons. The sound set his pulse pounding.

Then the engine noise grew louder amid a fresh flurry of gunshots. At the curve of the road near the mansion, headlight beams lit up a piece of empty ground, swept past it, flaring into full view.

"Get behind the wheel!" Asrat told the truck driver.

What the man was doing standing with hands in pockets beside the driver's door was a complete mystery to the officer. An infuriating mystery. Asrat helped the man aboard with a swift kick in the ass.

Headlights grew closer. Two pairs. Truck leading. Car following. They illuminated the ambush zone.

"Start it up!" the major general shouted, slamming his fist against the door.

The driver hit the starter and the engine caught at once. He revved it and released the hand brake.

Not a moment too soon.

The two-vehicle convoy was almost on top of them.

"Roll it! Roll it!" Asrat bellowed.

The driver tried to obey. He shifted with a screech of grinding gears, then popped the clutch and held on for dear life. The truck jumped from the curb out toward the middle of the intersection. It took one jump, then it hopped, then it stopped. Stalled. The flustered driver had put the truck in the wrong gear by accident.

"Idiot!" Asrat shouted.

The man cranked up the starter. Again the engine caught on the first try.

Asrat could see it was already too late. The 6x6 was swerving to avoid the collision, making for the narrow path still open to it. The major general yelled to his men to stand back and prepare to fire. As they lined up in the middle of the intersection, he grabbed an AK out of one of the soldier's hands and shouldered it.

The money truck sideswiped the front end of the major general's truck, throwing a breaking wave of glass and metal bits over the street in its wake.

Asrat opened fire on the speeding truck. The AK bucked against his shoulder and a stream of bright brass vomited from the ejection port. He could not hear the sound of his own shooting for the ear-splitting full-auto din around him. He turned with the truck, trigger pinned, trying to swing past the bed and onto the cab. The truck moved too fast. He emptied the clip into the backside of the vehicle.

His own truck lunged forward, the driver having recovered from the crash. Before the man could close off the escape route, the following car squeaked through. The truck driver crashed head-on into a wall of bricks.

The gate was closed, but the sheep had already fled.

Asrat watched in impotent fury as the Mercedes fishtailed through the intersection. It swung wide left to avoid the corner of the building, offering its whole unprotected side to the assembled troops. Unfortunately, almost all of Asrat's men had done the same thing he had, expended all their ammunition on the money truck. There was no time to remove the empty clips and reload.

The number of steel-cored bullets turned loose on the retreating car, a target that concentrated fire might have stopped, were few and far between.

"Major General!" one of his men shouted, pointing over their truck's ruined front bumper, back in the direction of the Crusade mansion.

Another pair of headlights.

Another truck barreling down on them.

Asrat swore aloud. He yelled at his men to take position behind the barricade, ripping the spent mag from his AK and snatching a full one from a nearby soldier's belt pack. He cracked it in place, seating it with a hell of a hand slap and released the bolt, chambering a live round.

He stared at the approaching headlights. He didn't know who was in the second truck. The men who had tried to take the money from Heiss? Or Heiss pursuing them to get it back? He hoped it was Heiss, but he really didn't give a good goddamn.

The barrier was in place.
His men had reloaded.
This truck would not get away.

16

One look at the road ahead told Barrabas that his luck had indeed changed. For the worse.

From the bed of the 6x6 he watched through two layers of dirty glass, the truck cab's rear window and the front windshield, as the trap was sprung. For a split second it didn't look like any of them, the money truck, the Mercedes or the SOBs were going to get through. Then, inexplicably the rolling barricade stopped just short of sealing off the street.

And the two lead vehicles squeezed past.

When O'Toole saw the brake lights flash in front of him, he instinctively took his foot off the gas. The heavy truck slowed at once.

Barrabas pounded on the rear window with his fist. "Go! Go!" he shouted. If they had any chance at all of getting by, that chance was growing slimmer by the moment. The ambush truck was shutting off the gap.

"Hang on, fat man," Liam said, tromping the pedal to the floorboard. The engine responded with an immediate, sustained bellow; it was the only thing immediate that happened. The truck was geared for torque not acceleration. Accordingly, it went nowhere with a great deal of ruckus. It was only after O'Toole threw a few up-gear speed shifts, his left leg pumping frantically to make the necessary double-clutches, that the behemoth broke the inertia of its own weight. After that, it picked up speed rapidly.

It was white knuckle time for Walker Jessup. Way up front in the shotgun seat, he had a perfect view of the solid obstacle they were rushing toward. The rest of the SOBs still had the thrill of discovery to look forward to.

"What is it?" Lee Hatton said, moving beside Barrabas at the window. "Oh, God!" she exclaimed. Not only was the street blocked, but armed men swarmed behind the barrier.

"Hit it, Liam!" Barrabas yelled. "Hit it dead center! Go for the gas tank!" Then to all of the SOBs he said, "Bail out! Bail the hell out!"

It was going to be real tight.

Hayes and Hatton dropped over the tailgate, landing on their feet and rolling to dissipate the shock. Barrabas, Billy Two and Nanos followed. The SOBs scrambled to their feet and the truck roared away without them.

Autofire winked orange from the intersection; ComBloc slugs sliced the air inches over their heads.

"Jump you fools!" Barrabas yelled at the back of the 6x6 as it roared away from them. O'Toole and Jessup were still in the truck's cab.

They couldn't hear him. They were having a discussion. The barrier was less than a hundred fifty feet away.

"Go on, jump!" Liam told the fat man.

Jessup shook his head, reaching across the dash to grab his custom wheelgun. He stuck it in his pants pocket. "I go when you go."

"Fucking A!" the Irish-American yelped as steel-cored bullets spidershattered the windshield, thudding into and through the back wall of the cab. He instinctively threw up a forearm to protect his eyes from the flying glass.

"That does it," O'Toole said, opening the driver's door.

The barrier was ninety feet away.

He and Jessup hit the asphalt at the same instant. Jessup hit it rather harder than O'Toole, however. Neither of them had time to get up before the truck-on-truck impact. It was just as well. If they had managed to rise, the explosion would've put them right back down again.

It didn't come instantly.

First there was the crash of metal on metal, the squeal of five pairs of tires forced to move suddenly sideways from a pile-driver perpendicular blow. The SOB's 6x6 slammed the ambush truck out into the middle of the intersection. In the process it ruptured the vehicle's gas tank and the fluid gushed out over the street, gushed even as the tangled trucks continued to slide, scraping, sparking steel to steel.

The explosion came when gasoline vapors ignited. A terrible air-sucking fireball that engulfed both 6x6s. The fuel that had spilled over the intersection became a burning lava lake. Soldiers caught wading in it died, their panicked final cries lost in the roar of the blaze.

Then the second gas tank blew.

The SOB's truck jumped at the rocking boom. Flames leapt a hundred feet in the air.

O'Toole covered his head as the burning debris rained down. He couldn't afford to cover for long. He was out in the open. So was Jessup. The Texan was lying in the street on his side, a beached whale. As Liam struggled to his feet, the wind shifted and swept a pall of black smoke over him. Coughing, he recovered his SMG and stumbled over to the fat man.

"Come on, get up!" O'Toole said, shaking his arm.

Jessup groaned.

O'Toole could see troops skirting the big ball of flame. They would be in position to shoot in a minute or two. Behind him, some forty yards back, the other five SOBs had started to run to their aid.

"No, goddammit!" he yelled, waving them off. "Keep back! I can handle it!" He was glad to see the colonel stop the rescue attempt and direct his friends to take cover. There was no sense in all of them getting killed for the fat man.

He bent over Jessup and shouted down at him. "Get up! Get up or I'm going to goddamn leave you! I sure as hell can't carry you!"

The only response was another groan.

It occurred to O'Toole that the fat man must've hit his head when he landed on the street. He lifted Jessup's head from the road and slid his hand underneath it. His fingers came back sticky wet with blood. "This is the pits," he muttered.

He shouldered his SMG, then took hold of both of Jessup's wrists, rolling him over on his back. If he couldn't lift the guy to safety, he would damn well have to drag him.

It actually wasn't so bad once he got going. He had to move backward, though, using the powerful muscles of his legs. As O'Toole hauled Jessup's unconscious body along, it shuddered and shook like three hundred fifty pounds of pudding.

Liam had just got him up over the curb when the bullets started flying again, cutting chips out of the sidewalk. He couldn't return fire. If he stopped, let go of Jessup and unslung his submachine gun, they were both going to be dead. Cursing a blue streak, he summoned heretofore untapped sources of strength. He jerked the fat man across the strip of sidewalk and onto the scrub lot that bordered the corner building. The bullets kept coming as he backed into the boondocks.

As far as defensive potential went, the terrain purely sucked.

To his rear, some fifty yards away, was the perimeter wall of one of the Crusade's neighboring mansions. Thirty yards in the other direction was the street corner, the burning trucks, the shooters and the side of a two-story office building. The scrub lot was flat, featureless except for weeds and bushes ranging from ankle to chest height.

O'Toole kept looking over his shoulder to make sure he didn't trip. He didn't have a clue where he was going; he just wanted to put some distance between himself and the muzzles of all those autorifles.

Jessup moaned again as Liam slithered him around a boulder. Bathed in sweat, his back and arms thoroughly strained, bullets whizzing every which way, O'Toole didn't want to hear so much as a whimper from the super heavyweight.

"Hey, button it," he told the totally oblivious man. When Jessup kept up his groaning, he said, "You know, I don't mind putting my rear on the line to save a guy's life. I'd do it for almost anybody. What bothers me about this particular situation is that with the load I'm draggin' for you I could be saving a family of four.''

O'Toole stopped dragging when he thought he'd gone far enough. He got down on all fours and backed into a tight little grove of bushes, pulling the limp body in after him. The random sprays of gunfire coming his way suddenly stopped. In the near distance, on the other side of the burning intersection, one hell of a firefight raged on. It occurred to him that the firing was coming from the wrong direction. Definitely a busy night for the gangsters of Addis.

He lay on his belly and checked out the silenced MP5 SD3. As he worked, he said to the supine Texan by his side, ''If we live through this, Jessup, and you don't go get your maw wired shut out of pure gratitude to my aching back, I swear I'm going to buy the biggest tube of epoxy I can find and...''

Liam shut up.

The shooters were on the edge of the scrub near the corner. Over the hiss of the fire, the automatic weapons clatter, he could hear them talking, getting their act together. Then they started moving through the bush in formation, snapping twigs, brushing aside branches. Jesus, he thought, now I know how a quail feels. He closed his eyes and listened as hard as he could, trying to judge their number and the speed of their approach.

He only came to one conclusion—there were too damn many of them.

Jessup groaned again. Then he moved his head and tried to raise up on his elbows. And for his trouble he got a face full of branches.

"Easy, now," Liam said softly, grabbing the fat man's arm. He squeezed it hard, digging his fingers deep into the doughy flesh to make sure he had the man's undivided attention. "Lay real still. We're about to be overrun by some guys in green uniforms."

Jessup let his head drop back to the dirt.

"That's the way," O'Toole told him. "Leave everything to me."

A stick snapped off to his left. Fabric brushed over the tip of a bush straight ahead. He couldn't see a thing over the sights of his silenced SMG.

Come on, come on, he thought. Show yourselves! Give me a target and I'll give you a big surprise.

As if in answer to his plea, three pairs of boots stepped into view. The surprise was O'Toole's. They were so close that one of them kicked sand in his face.

MAJOR GENERAL ASRAT was no fool. He knew his position was about to be rammed. He stopped shooting at the truck cab and, screaming at the top of his lungs, ordered his soldiers away from the barricade. As he turned to look back, he saw two men drop from the cab of the onrushing enemy 6x6.

He dove away from the nose of his own truck, around the corner, just before the moment of collision. He dove and landed on his stomach. The impact shook the ground under him, rattled the organs in his chest. He rolled to his side to look back.

The trucks were sliding to the center of the crossroads.

He smelled gas.

Everything went red.

And there was no air to breathe.

Scrambling to his feet, he ran from the leaping flames. Behind him there was a terrible bass *whooomp!* And the blast concussion laid him out flat.

He looked back again. A towering spire of flame reached up for the stars. At its base it filled the entire intersection. The two huge 6x6s were dwarfed by the size of the conflagration, like toy trucks caught in a bonfire.

The machines were not the only ones caught. Human comets raced away from the central blaze. Arms waving, bodies trailing long tongues of fire.

Asrat shook his head to clear the image from his mind. Some of his men were all right. He could see them up ahead. He pushed to his feet and ran up to them. They looked stunned.

"The men who did this are there," he told them, pointing toward the street. "I saw them jump off the truck before it hit. Follow me and we will make them pay."

He led a half-dozen troopers back to the intersection.

"There!" he said. "See?"

They could all see. A short, stocky man pulling a huge fat man by the arms. They didn't wait for the order to shoot. They knelt and began firing wildly.

As they did so, from behind them, more gunfire started up. Asrat looked back. The raging fire obscured his view of whatever was going on. Whoever was shooting wasn't shooting at them. And that's all that he cared about. He put rifle to shoulder and sent a burst of 7.62x39 slugs into the scrub lot after the retreating figures.

"Hold your fire!" he ordered his men. They were reloading and resuming their barrage even though their targets had completely disappeared into the brush. "Hold your fire. We've got them, now. There's no place for them to run. Follow me."

He took the soldiers to the edge of the lot and set up a skirmish line. "Keep the line as even as you can," he told them as they started their sweep. "And shoot anything that moves."

They had only gone about ten yards into the scrub when a trooper on Asrat's right called out. The major general hurried over to him.

"See what I've found, sir?" the private said kneeling down and patting the soft ground.

Asrat smiled. The fleeing duo was leaving a wide trail to follow. The man being dragged was so heavy he plowed a furrow in the dirt and crushed down the vegetation. Where the body track ended they would find one of them for sure. They might even find both, if the man who was doing the dragging refused to leave his injured comrade.

The major general pulled in the ends of the skirmish line, tightening the formation, so when they made contact they could quickly encircle and cut off a further retreat.

The only problem was the lack of light.

The deeper they probed the scrub lot, the farther they got from the fire, the darker it got. That, coupled with the belly height of most of the bushes, made it impossible to see more than a few feet ahead. The deeper they penetrated, the slower they had to go.

Asrat could feel his own nerves beginning to tighten up. He knew the man doing the pulling couldn't have gone much farther into the brush without a rest. Somewhere, just ahead, he was waiting, probably armed, certainly ready to kill. The possibility of being caught in an ambush loomed large. Bunched together as they were, his soldiers could be easily chopped down by flanking fire.

He silently signaled for a stop, touching the shoulders of the men on his left and right who, in turn, touched the men next to them. At Asrat's direction, they huddled, kneeling beside a fallen tree.

He spoke quickly and softly. They would split up into two groups. One would continue to follow the track. The other would parallel at a distance of thirty feet, ready to counter any ambush that might be set up.

The major general waved the cannon fodder of the tracking team into the thick scrub. He took his place at the head of the shadowing unit.

His nerves felt better already.

O'TOOLE HELD HIS BREATH, keeping perfectly still. He didn't dare wipe off the grit that had been kicked in his face. The guys in green were so close he could smell the leather of their boots. His problem wasn't with the three right under his nose. Even though his angle of attack stunk and the bush was in his line of fire, he was confident he could handle them. His problem was with the others. The ones he couldn't see. Once he started shooting they would have him. The silenced weapon he held wouldn't silence screams or answering gunshots.

One pair of boots moved, stepping out of his sight. It was back after a moment. O'Toole could hear them whispering but he couldn't make sense of what they were saying. It was in some Ethiopian dialect.

Then the decision-making was taken completely out of his hands.

One of the men knelt down and peered under the bush where Liam and Jessup lay hiding.

O'Toole had no choice. He pushed the barrel of the H&K forward and mashed the trigger. The curious soldier's head was less than a foot from the muzzle when the weapon discharged. The muzzle flash lit up the guy's face like a strobe. A hole roughly 9 mm in diameter appeared in the center of his forehead. The afterimage of his astonished agony burned into Liam's brain. Then the soldier slumped down, cheek to earth, as if he were suddenly overcome with an urge to sleep.

The man's comrades knew a silenced shot when they heard one. They gasped and stepped back.

Liam swung his sights up and fired full auto. Parabellum brass bounced off the branches and hit him in the head as he emptied the magazine into what he guessed were the center torsos of the standing figures. He guessed right because there were two thuds and suddenly he was looking at the heels of their boots.

Over his head, the sustained muzzle blast had set fire to the lower limbs of the bush. Telling anyone who was interested exactly where he and Jessup were hanging out.

"Don't move," he told the fat man, then he slithered out from under the shrub and took off at top speed. He made a lot of noise. He made it on purpose. His aim was to draw pursuit away from Jessup. As he ran he stripped out the spent SMG clip. He was trying to fit a fresh one to the magazine well when he was spotted.

There was a shout off to his left and then shots. The slugs passed so close he could feel their wind. Freight trains hurtling past his ears. O'Toole dove to the dirt and crawled under the nearest bush. The soldiers stopped firing for a few seconds, and O'Toole almost thought they had lost his position in the dark.

No such luck.

They were just trying to get the best angle on him.

When they had it, the firing resumed.

And it was horrendous. And accurate.

The troopers shot down into the ground, bracketing him with concentrated autofire, putting him right in the middle of their beaten zone. Slugs rained all around him, throwing up dirt, shaking the ground.

''Sweet Jesus!'' O'Toole moaned over the clattering din, frantically belly-crawling as fast as he could.

It was go crazy time.

He couldn't see a damned thing. He didn't know which way he was going. And the bullets kept coming. He knew he was going to get hit. He knew it in his guts.

Even though he expected it, even though he'd been shot many times before, once earlier that very same day, when it finally did happen, it was a big surprise. It was always a big surprise. A bullet wound was something a guy never got used to.

His right leg kicked to the side, slammed by a slug through the back of his thigh. The impact numbed him from toes to shoulder. Then the numb peeled away and it started to hurt. The pain made him bury his face in the dirt.

The shooting petered out above him.

The troopers were reloading.

He had to get it together. He rolled to his left and felt the wound. Through and through. Not much blood. Missed the bone. No way could he run on the leg, though. He was stuck.

When the shooting started up again, he stayed put. He wasn't about to go out on his belly, with a bullet in the back. He sat up in a little open space between some brush and watched for the muzzle flashes.

When the autorifles barked at him, he swung his own weapon on target, aiming just above the blinking orange. The zip-thwack, zip-thwack of the silenced, low-velocity parabellums told him he had hit meat. One of the lights blinked out.

Steel cores kicked dirt into his lap as he chopped down the second shooter. Then the firing stopped.

Three guns.

He had counted three. The last guy must have figured out what was happening and dropped down. Liam grimaced. One on one was his kind of game. He could have crawled away if he'd wanted to. Slipped off into the dark and safety. He could have, but he didn't.

O'Toole crawled for the spot he had last seen gunflash, trailing his wounded leg. It was throbbing now. The pain made him hurry, perhaps too much.

As he crossed an open spot a voice called out to him. He didn't recognize the word, but the meaning was obvious. Freeze. He froze. The guy had gotten position on him.

"Speak English," he told the shadow.

"American? Throw your gun away."

When O'Toole did so, the man stood up and cautiously approached him from the rear.

"An American terrorist," the man said with unconcealed glee. "This will make the headlines."

Liam turned to look at his captor. He could see the gleaming metal insignia on the shirt collar. A major general, no less. "I don't give interviews," he said.

"Dead men rarely do."

The officer aimed his AK at O'Toole's neck. "Have you got any last words?"

"Yeah, I got two of 'em," Liam said. "Fuck you!"

Zip-thwack, zip-thwack, zip-thwack.

The major general dropped like all his strings had been cut.

No staggers.

No gestures.

No words.

One second he was alive and a threat; the next, he was dead on his feet. When he hit the ground beside O'Toole, he no longer had a face.

Liam sat up, scanning the dim brush line. Five figures rose from the bushes. Five familiar figures.

"Cut it a little close, didn't you?" he said to the rest of the SOBs.

"Loved your famous last words," Nanos said as he and the others hurried over to Liam's side.

"Real poetic," Billy Two agreed. "Practically moved me to tears."

"Do me a favor, bozos," Liam said, through gritted teeth. "When I finally do buy it, put 'em on my tombstone."

17

Lt. Hailu listened gleefully to the first crackling sounds of battle. He and two of the Soviet military "advisors" to his nation, Captains Vlanov and Ushensko, stood on the roof of a two-story building overlooking both Major General Asrat's ambush and their own.

Vlanov, a short, bald, cube of a man, conferred in Russian with his comrade, then told the lieutenant, "My friend, Ushensko, is concerned that your superior might have already discovered our plan. He doesn't want to lose his valuable, seasoned troops in a debacle."

Lt. Hailu grinned broadly and shook his head. "Tell him he has nothing to worry about. My superior delegated the planning of his ambush to me. Which, you can imagine, made it much easier for me to plan a second trap that cannot possibly fail. You will not lose a single man, I guarantee it."

Ushensko listened to the translation, a scowl on his florid face. He was not convinced.

"You understand the operating principle of the first ambush?" Hailu said. "That the truck must completely cross the road to block it off?"

Vlanov nodded for both himself and his comrade.

"Well, the truck will not cross the road. I have arranged for this to happen."

Vlanov translated. Ushensko barked back a question.

"He says you are talking around the point. What if Asrat knows we are waiting?"

"He doesn't, I assure you. But it makes no difference, either way. You see, once the truck with the money gets past his position, he will have to pursue it. The truck, because of its high rate of speed and poor maneuverability, will only be able to continue in the direction it is already traveling. A direction that will bring it under our guns. When Asrat pursues, he will be under our guns as well."

Ushensko said something, his eyes glittering with menace.

"For your sake, my friend," Vlanov told Hailu, "I hope things go as smoothly as you say."

The lieutenant shrugged off the threat. He knew Asrat. And he knew how to beat him.

The money convoy appeared in the distance. A truck with a tailing car.

Hailu watched in astonishment as a second truck appeared behind the car.

"One truck," Vlanov said. "You told us only one truck."

The lieutenant didn't respond. He had a terrible thought: what if Asrat had secretly arranged for a second truckload of combat troops to be brought in? A kind of backup to the men already stationed at the roadblock? Another thirty soldiers loyal to Asrat could disrupt, if not destroy his plan to take all the money.

"The ambush truck is moving," Vlanov said.

There was a touch of elation in the man's voice as he continued to narrate what had all the appearances of an impending disaster. The pleasure the Russian got from relating bad news irritated the lieutenant, no end.

"And it's stopping! See?" Hailu said, defiantly.

The money truck and the trailing car got by. Then, according to plan, the ambush truck sealed off the street. The only thing it was meant to prevent was a successful retreat by Asrat and his men. Due to unforeseen developments it fulfilled another purpose, as well. It kept the second truck from going through the intersection. It did not, however, keep it from trying.

"Oh!" Ushensko exclaimed as collision became fireball.

"Now, we will see," Vlanov said, pointing at the escaping truck and car.

Lt. Hailu had his confidence back. If the second truck contained Asrat troops, they were no longer a consideration. They were charcoal. He watched spellbound as his own plan unfolded below.

On the left side of the street, parked with its tail-gate facing the conflagration, was a Soviet-made 6x6. The truck was so wide that it took up almost half the road. Idling just around the right corner, ready to make a quick right turn into the only available lane of traffic was an identical truck.

As the money truck swerved to miss the parked truck, the idling one made its turn.

Suddenly there was no place for the money truck to go.

The second collision in the space of a block was a double head-on. It would have been much more severe if the driver of the money truck hadn't slammed on his brakes at the very last instant. Severe to the truck, that is; it couldn't have been any more severe for the driver. The impact hurled him and the cab passenger straight through the front windshield. Their bodies sprawled onto the truck's hood, feet still hooked over the jagged hole in the glass.

Behind the stopped Crusade '85 truck, the trailing car hit its own brakes. The driver was quite good. He spun the car 180 degrees and brought it to a stop with its rear deck under the back bumper of the Crusade '85 truck.

The money truck was wheel to wheel, bed to bed, with the parked Soviet vehicle.

"Get them!" Hailu shouted down from the rooftop.

The Russian advisors threw back the canvas cover that concealed their presence in the back of the parked 6x6. They did not give Karl Heiss's men the chance to do the same. They fired, virtually point blank from one bed to the other, shooting through the canvas walls.

"Beautiful," Hailu said, watching the clouds of cordite smoke rise, seeing the flicking yellow flames of muzzle blast.

The driver of the Mercedes wanted no part of it. He laid twin patches of smoking rubber, peeling back in the direction he had just come. Some of the "advisors" turned their weapons on him, but it was already too late. He skirted the lake of fire to rip a squealing left turn and vanish around the corner.

Meanwhile, the "advisors" shot the back of the truck to ribbons and splinters. A couple of the hapless mercenaries managed to jump out the back, but once on the street there was nowhere for them to run and nothing for them to do. But die.

The whole scenario, from Hailu's first sighting of the convoy to the Russian order to cease fire, had taken no more than three minutes.

It was the most profitable three minutes in the lieutenant's young life.

The two Soviet captains were not displeased, either. Although Comrade Ushensko still refused to smile.

"What did I tell you?" Hailu said. "Never a doubt, was there?"

"What is that shooting?" Vlanov asked.

It was coming from the other side of the intersection. At least half a dozen automatic weapons were burning up ammunition at maximum rounds per minute.

"It has nothing to do with our great victory," the lieutenant said. "Shall we go count our fortunes?"

As they descended the building's fire escape, Ushensko muttered something to Vlanov. The lieutenant paused on the stairs for yet another translation.

"He doesn't like that shooting, either."

LOOKING OVER the Mercedes's front seat as Karl Heiss swung the car off the sidewalk and onto pavement, Dr. Lalarva forgot all about anticipated pleasures. He let out a low and baleful moan. The car was doing seventy miles an hour and accelerating, and the street in front of them had suddenly turned into a dead end.

The money truck cut to the left, trying to avoid the parked 6x6's rear end. Then its brake lights came on and stayed on, all those big wheels locked in a screeching skid that climaxed in an abrupt and complete stop. The cessation of forward motion was so violent that the double back sets of wheels jumped from the ground. And the tailgate dropped down.

Heiss slammed his own brakes, putting the sedan into a sickening four-wheel drift. For a moment it looked like they were going to crash into the leading truck sideways.

"Oh, Lord," Lalarva gasped, clawing at the seat back as he fought the force of gravity.

Heiss didn't turn into the skid the way Lalarva had been taught in high-school Driver's Ed. He turned away from it, making the car rotate another ninety degrees, making it slide ass-backward while he stood on the brake pedal with both feet.

Lalarva could see the 6x6's tailgate rushing up at him. It looked like it was going to take his head off! He let go of the seat back and was thrown to the floor.

Then the car stopped.

Lalarva looked through the car's back window to see the edge of the metal tailgate touching the glass. "God, that was close!" he exclaimed.

Automatic weapons cut loose. Not potshooting, but serious sustained fire less than five feet away. The hammering din was unreal.

Lalarva was right there to see the show. He saw the white soldiers in unmarked uniforms, saw them emptying their weapons into the bed of the Crusade '85 truck. He saw inside the bed of the truck as well. Heiss's mercenaries were being cut to pieces, literally. So were the bags containing the money.

"The money!" he wailed.

"Shit!" Heiss snarled, popping the clutch and flooring the gas.

Lalarva was thrown back to the floor and held there by the crushing pressure of the acceleration. He dragged himself up to look over the seat and instantly wished he hadn't.

"The fire! You're heading for the fire!" he cried.

Heiss knew where he was heading. He slashed the wheel left, skidding through the verge of the inferno, skidding past the twisted heaps of wreckage. He fought and beat the four-wheel slide through the puddle of flaming gas, then streaked away, turbo howling blue blazes.

"We're on fire!" Lalarva yelled, pointing at the car's back end.

Indeed, flames from splattered fuel curled up over the trunk lid.

"It'll burn out on its own," Heiss told him.

Lalarva watched it do just that. He sank back into the seat, his eyes bulging with fright and shock behind his purple-tinted lenses. "What happened?" he gasped.

"We just lost thirty million dollars, you asshole."

"Who were all those people with guns?"

Heiss said nothing.

"You know them?" Lalarva demanded shrilly. "You called one of them by name back there. You said he had an army. I heard you say it!"

Heiss searched the rearview mirror for pursuit and seeing none, slacked off the gas. The speedometer, which had been pinned on the extreme right, dropped back to a sedate 110 miles per hour.

Heiss spoke from between clenched teeth. "I know a son of a bitch with white hair who's supposed to be dead and buried." Heiss slammed down his fist on the padded dash. "Damn the bastard to hell! He isn't dead and he isn't buried. And yes, he's got himself an army. All handpicked dirty bastards. He did it. He took us for every last dime."

Lalarva's confusion was almost complete. As Heiss continued to rant about the white-haired man, he dropped back to the seat and shut his mind to the raving. Three things had happened that shouldn't have happened: the attack on the mansion, the second roadblock, and the loss of the money to persons unknown. It was conceivable that it all had been engineered by this Barrabas. But Heiss was so rabid on the subject that it made Lalarva think the "white-haired man" was part of some kind of paranoid delusion of his: the all-seeing, all-knowing, all-powerful enemy.

"I could've killed him myself in Sri Lanka," Heiss was saying. "I should've killed him."

Lalarva's concerns were with the present, not the past.

"What are we going to do, now?" he asked.

Heiss stopped his tirade and glared at him in the rearview mirror.

"We've got to do something. We can't stay here in Addis. We can't get the money back. There's nobody to fight for us. All your men are dead."

Heiss looked back at the road.

"I say we go on to the refugee camp as planned," Lalarva told him. "I make the live pitch for more money, then we cut over the border into Sudan where we can stop and think things out. What do you say? We've got the travel documents. The camera crews will be waiting there for me, anyway."

After a moment, Heiss nodded. "Maybe we can still salvage something out of this mess," he said.

Lalarva's thoughts precisely, except for the "we." When they got close to the camp, "we" would cease to exist.

LT. HAILU WATCHED WITH PLEASURE at the way the Soviet "advisors" got down to business. It was true that some few among his countrymen complained about the influx of milk-faced foreigners from the East. They blamed the Russians for turning all the young women into prostitutes, the young men into cowards. They said the Russians were tightfisted cheapskates who stole their coffee crops, who never gave alms to beggars, who, with their relatively "hard" currency, always bought everything new and then wore it with the price tag showing, to rub the natives' noses in it. As a people they smelled uniformly bad and despite this, or perhaps because of it, they always acted aloof and superior.

All of that might have been true, but when push came to shove, the Soviets knew how to do a job.

Hailu watched as the Russians sorted through the wreckage in the bed of the Crusade '85 truck, pitching the useless debris out onto the road. The larger pieces, torsos and the like, were handled by a pair of the soldiers working together, in the true spirit of international brotherhood.

As the heap of bodies grew on the street, the stack of grain sacks became visible. Some of the money had fallen from slashes in the bags, cuts made by the barrage of bullets. The advisors were extremely fastidious. They wiped the blood off each bill and then stuffed it back into the sack.

The dead driver and passenger had been hauled off the truck hood and a Soviet soldier was behind the wheel, starting the engine. He shouted a warning, then backed the truck up a couple of feet, freeing it from the bumper of the Soviet vehicle. It came away with a screech of protesting metal, both from the truck alongside as well as the truck in front.

They worked like ants, Lt. Hailu thought. Busy, busy ants. The parked truck that had served as a shooting platform was also started up.

"No complaints, I take it, Captain Vlanov?" Hailu said as the man stepped up to him.

"Everything is fine. We will be finished here in a very few minutes."

"And Captain Ushensko? The shooting he didn't like has stopped."

"He is aware of that."

"Did I tell you both there was absolutely nothing to worry about?"

Vlanov knew when he was being ragged. He did not answer the question. Instead, he growled an order at one of the men in the back of the money truck. The man was bent over a gore-spattered grain bag and did not understand the command. He walked across the truck bed and stepped out onto the tailgate so he could get it right.

He got it all right.

From the direction of the burning wrecks came the sound of a single gunshot. Heavy caliber. Like a thunderclap. And the slug whined overhead.

The soldier on the tailgate took a 180-grain AP round through the belly. It knocked him flat on his butt. It knocked the air from his lungs. As the advisor clutched his wound, gasping, a second and third shot rang out.

Hailu hit the dirt.

The two Russian captains did likewise.

The man on the tailgate couldn't duck. The bullets had his name on them. They took his head off. In chunks.

Gunfire from all quarters hammered them, scattering the Soviet troops. Captain Ushensko drew a Makarov from his belt and aimed it at Lt. Hailu's chest.

"What! What are you doing?"

Vlanov raised his face from the filthy street and, in a voice dripping acid, said, "Everything is all right. There is absolutely nothing to worry about."

18

Over the sounds of nearby gunfire Barrabas and the others heard a car straining, winding out in high gear, red-lined to the max.

"Somebody's in a hurry," Nanos said as he and Billy Two helped O'Toole across the scrub lot.

"In a hurry to be elsewhere and who can blame 'em?" O'Toole said.

"Are you sure you left Jessup over here?" Dr. Hatton asked him.

"Yeah, doc, it's not far. We should be able to find him, no sweat. I left him under a burning bush."

"Like Moses," the Greek suggested.

"Moses?" Billy Two said in bewilderment.

"You know, the baby found in the burning bullrushes."

"Alex, you got it wrong," the Indian said. "Moses found the Ten Commandments under the burning bullrushes."

"Yeah, well, I was close wasn't I?"

O'Toole groaned as his foot hit a rock and excruciating pain lanced all the way up his side. He was in no mood for fractured tales from the Old Testament. "You guys are so dumb," he said, shaking his head. "I bet you can't even tell me what the First Commandment is."

"Go on, Billy, tell 'im."

"No, this is your big chance to show off."

"I give up," Nanos said at once.

"Me, too," Starfoot said.

"I'll bet you don't know, either, O'Toole," Hayes chimed in from the rear.

The Irish-American straightened as he hopped along between the two much-larger men. "Hey, those are fightin' words," he said. "Do you know how many times Sister made me write the first Commandment on the blackboard? I'll tell you something, it's burned into my memory."

"Like your first two-week drunk?" Nanos said.

"No, I don't remember that at all."

"Third grade was a long time ago," Billy told him.

"You want to hear the first Commandment or not?"

"Do we have any choice?" Dr. Hatton asked.

"The first Commandment is: Thou shalt not kill."

Lee Hatton shook her head in despair. Where did these guys go to Sunday School, she wondered, some sleazy bar and grill?

"We all know where O'Toole's headed after he bites the big one," Hayes said.

"You and me both, brother. Straight to hell."

The bush was no longer burning when they got to Jessup, but as he was sitting up, there was no problem in spotting him. Lee Hatton checked out his head injury.

"He'll be all right," she told Barrabas.

The shooting over on the other side of the intersection stopped. The only audible sound was the whistle and hiss of the big blaze.

"Aren't there any fire trucks in this place?" Nanos asked.

"They'll be here," Jessup said. "In another half hour."

"What now, Colonel?" O'Toole said.

Barrabas was watching the column of flames. Bits of burning matter climbed up into the night sky, blown above the peak of the fire by the rising heat.

"I wonder what caused all the commotion over there?" he said. "I mean on the other side of the ambush."

"Something to do with the money?" Billy suggested.

"I'd bet on it," Barrabas said. "I think we'll go over that way and take a look. We can't hang around here much longer, anyway. We need some transportation out of the disaster zone before the police arrive."

"I hate to bring it up, Colonel," Liam said, "but I don't know if I can walk that far."

"Don't worry about it, O'Toole," Billy Two said. "I'll carry you. Come on, get up on my back."

O'Toole climbed on, piggy back, locking his arms around the Indian's neck.

"I don't feel so hot, either, Barrabas," Jessup confessed after they had gone a few steps.

The group paused.

"Don't look at me!" Nanos warned them.

"And we thought you were such a big, strong, macho kind of guy, Alex," Lee Hatton said.

"Or so he led us to believe," Hayes said.

"Do it, Greek," Barrabas told him. "We can't afford to waste any more time."

Nanos hunkered down grudgingly. As Jessup climbed on his broad and powerful back, he said, "Is there such a thing as rupture pay?"

Then he straightened.

"God, he looks like an ant carrying a cupcake!" Hayes exclaimed.

"Hey, Alex," Lee said, "you may start a whole new exercise fad. Pumping blubber."

"Move out," Barrabas told them, cutting the fun and games short. He understood the need for humor, though. It was a kind of tension release for all of them. They had survived so far, against all odds, and there was no guarantee the streak would hold. There was never a guarantee. They had to grab every moment of victory, squeeze all joy they could out of it, because a defeat on the battlefield, their place of business, could last for eternity.

Barrabas took point and led his SOBs back across the lot, toward the burning crossroads. They walked in silence, weapons ready. All of them were pumped, he could sense it. They thought they still had a chance to save the day.

Barrabas thought so, too.

He was a realist, but he believed in his own feelings. His combat intuition. The intangible, the unknowable had saved his butt many times before. He knew that the possibility of their getting a second shot at the Crusade '85 loot was slim and none; that the possibility of his getting a second shot at Karl Heiss was even worse. His past experience had taught him that once frightened, Heiss, like the cockroach, was capable of blinding spurts of speed. If his brain told him to forget it, his guts said, "Hang in a little longer. Play out the hand you've been dealt."

They approached the back wall of the corner building, fanning out automatically to offer a less tempting target. Barrabas led them parallel to the wall, out to the corner. He was the first to look around it. The heat from the fire hit him like a sledge; it was absolutely withering. Metal melted out in the intersection, melted and mixed with molten asphalt and charred humanity. The sheet of flame lit up the white-haired man's face. His black camo makeup was running, dripping down his neck like beads of India ink. His hooded eyes narrowed further as he strained to see past the waving curtain of flame and the shimmering wall of heat. There was no opposition at the crossroads. Everything, everyone was destroyed.

Barrabas turned back to his SOBs and said, "Come on."

They skirted the shrinking lake of fire, yellow flames still dancing, leaping. It was a place to hurry past. Bodies lay face down in the street, left beached, stranded as the fuel that had cooked them receded.

When they reached the corner on the other side of the street, Barrabas signaled for a stop. Billy Two and Nanos put down their passengers. All of the SOBs knelt down.

"We need some intel," Barrabas said. "Billy, you and Claude work your way down the street and see if you can find out what's ahead. Do it quick and do it right."

Hayes and Starfoot set off immediately. After they turned the corner, the Osage Navajo took the left side of the street and the black man the right.

After he had gone about ten yards, Hayes stopped in an alley between two low buildings and looked across the street. The Indian was nowhere in sight. Hayes smiled, shifting his MP5 SD3 to his left hand. Starfoot was over there, all right. Moving like the shadow of death.

Hayes peered around the edge of the building. He could see a pair of 6x6s jammed side by side. They took up the whole street, from sidewalk to sidewalk. There was barely enough room for a man to pass between them and the walls of the buildings that lined the street.

As he watched, a platoon of uniformed white men climbed out of the truck on the right. They were all armed. They approached the rear of the adjoining truck cautiously, as if expecting serious opposition. One man slipped up on the tailgate as another climbed from the bed of the left truck to the outside of its neighbor. The second soldier pulled aside the canvas cover as the first men moved inside. Then both of them were inside. After a moment the two of them appeared on the tailgate together. They were smiling and had wads of paper in their hands.

Greenbacks.

So the money was still up for grabs, Hayes thought.

Then someone grabbed him.

From behind.

Someone good.

Hayes knew that because he had broken necks before. The hands that gripped his shoulder and chin were professional. The sudden twist they give was professional, too. But Hayes had a neck like a bull. It didn't break easy. In the hands of a would-be killer, it didn't turn at all.

Claude caught the man's forearm, dropped to a squat and ducking his head, hurled himself into the wall. It was like football practice. The blocking sled. Only the ''sled'' in this case didn't move.

The lunge brought the top of the assassin's head into violent contact with the wall. His grip on Claude's shoulder weakened at once. Claude reared back and body-slammed the man to the ground.

A white guy in uniform.

Short, powerful arms.

A thick torso.

He didn't stay down long. He dove to the side, out of Hayes's reach and rolled to his feet, coming up in a fighting stance.

Claude swung his SMG around on its sling strap. The pistol grip was in his hand. ''What are you going to do, now, Ivan?'' he said, holding the fat, silenced barrel trained on the man's center chest.

The Russian touched his forehead. There was blood running down from a scalp wound. He smiled at Hayes.

"You know I'm going to blow you away, don't you?"

He knew. Which was why he feinted left, then charged straight at Hayes.

The black man fired twice, sidestepping like a matador. The parabellum slugs went through and through, smacking the wall behind. The Soviet soldier landed on his face and thrashed helplessly. There were two small exit wounds in the middle of his back.

"I would've done exactly the same thing," Hayes told him. Extending the H&K one-handed, like a pistol, he gave the man a quick, merciful coup de gras.

"Making new friends?" said a voice behind him.

Hayes pivoted, putting the SMG's sights on the speaker's camo-blackened face.

"Don't do that!" Hayes told Billy Two. "Don't ever do that again."

"Hey, I trust your judgment."

"I don't. Let's get back to the others. I've seen enough."

"The money truck?"

"Yeah, it looks like we're still in business."

After they had reported in, Barrabas devised the attack plan. He made it simple.

"Liam," he said, "since you and Jessup are not one hundred percent, you're going to provide a diversion for the main assault. I want each of you to take an FAL and set up on this corner and the one across the street. The rest of us will work all the way around the blocked part of the street and hit them from the other side. We'll split up into two teams. Hayes, you, Nanos and Billy will go around to the right. Lee, you and I will take the left. We'll synchronize watches. Everybody ready? Okay, mark! In four minutes, O'Toole and Jessup start shooting. Give it a second or two to sink in, then go for it."

"I'll take the far corner," Jessup said to O'Toole, slipping into the FN FAL's shoulder sling.

"Yeah, I'd appreciate that. The idea of humping overland with this leg does not appeal to me." Liam began setting up right there on the sidewalk, unfolding the FAL's bipod, laying out spare mags of ammo. "Shoot straight," he said.

The Texan nodded and started off. He was very much aware of what he owed O'Toole. The guy had saved his life twice. And in the process had gotten himself wounded, twice. Somehow, someway he would make it up to him. Walker Jessup always honored his obligations, no matter how disagreeable.

Something else Jessup was very much aware of: what an easy target he made. Big, slow, out of shape, he was made to order for a rookie sniper's first kill. He decided to take the long way around to his assigned position, keeping the flames and the wreckage between him and any possible hostile fire. It was a longer trip than he had bargained for. Luckily, he checked his watch at the midway point and realized that he was going to have to pick up speed if he was going to make position before the four minutes were up.

The Texan jogged for the first time in ten years.

It was a highly unpleasant experience. It made him sweat. It made his heart flutter and thud. It made the loose mass of his flesh jiggle and shake.

It confirmed his long-standing belief that as a man of action he was one hell of a string-puller, that the serious swashbuckling should be left to those with a normal ability to metabolize. Never again, he vowed, as rubber-legged he dragged tail over to the corner he had been assigned.

He unslung the FAL, opened the bipod and set it up as O'Toole had on the sidewalk. When he looked over his sights, he saw that his targets had decided to make things easier for him. They had put up some temporary lights at the scene of the action. Jessup could see the backs of both trucks and the men crawling all over them. They were throwing something out of the truck on the left. Throwing it into the street. It wasn't until an entire human carcass was so tossed that Jessup realized what they were discarding.

"Sweet mother," he muttered.

Jessup adjusted the FAL's rear sight and checked his watch again. Ten seconds. He put the machine rifle to his shoulder, snugging the butt-plate tight to the hollow of his arm, counting down in his head. He was lying prone, his elbows on the sidewalk. It was not comfortable, but he knew he wouldn't have to bear it for long.

Five seconds.

He put the front sight in the middle of the open rear of the truck on the left. A man was standing on the tailgate, talking to some other men on the street below him.

Jessup exhaled.

And tightened down on the trigger.

The FAL barked sharply, bucking against his shoulder. His man went down on the tailgate. Jessup followed and fired twice more.

Then he went looking for new targets.

ON HIS BELLY IN THE STREET, Lt. Hailu stared down the barrel of the Makarov, unable to fathom what was happening. An advisor fell to the street beside him, his chest cratered by a high-velocity slug. Similar bullets screamed past his head.

"You can't blame this on me!" he told the gun-wielding Ushensko. "I had nothing to do with it."

Vlanov, who had taken cover under the rear wheels of the money truck, said, "Captain Ushensko thinks you are a fool. And that your foolishness has caused the death of men whose boot soles you are not fit to lick."

"We still have the money!" Hailu protested. "I said I could put it in your lap, and I have. It's not my fault if you can't hold on to it."

Ushensko took aim.

"No!" Hailu shouted, jumping to his feet. He was not about to lie there and be shot like a dog. He ran like a madman, dove under the truck on the right, then slithered for its front end. The whole time he expected to hear a gunshot at his back, the shot that would kill him. He reached the front of the truck, scrambled out from under the bumper and dashed for the corner. As he turned it, he saw three men running toward him, all in black-face, all armed. He slid to a stop and changed directions.

Again he fully expected to hear a fatal gunshot at his back.

He got a terrible surprise, when, with no accompanying sound, something smashed into his back and five terrible holes sprang open in the front of his chest. He fell to his knees, then his face. His cheek pressed against the sidewalk, blood pouring from his mouth and nose, the last thing he heard was the footfalls of his killers as they ran past.

NANOS DIDN'T LIKE shooting a guy in the back, but there were times when some of the moral niceties had to be put aside in favor of survival. This particular guy had turned, gone rabbit, heading back to deliver a warning to his pals who just happened to outnumber the SOBs by five to one. No, sir, the Greek thought, as he sprinted by the crumpled body on the ground, you did the wrong thing and I did the right thing.

Hayes led Nanos and Billy Two up to the corner. O'Toole and Jessup were doing their job, all right. Peering around the edge was like playing chicken with a buzz saw. Their .308 caliber AP slugs howled by, ricocheting off the trucks, off the building walls, off the street.

"Holy shit!" Nanos said as he saw just how many Russians they were up against. He ducked his head back and conferred with Billy and Hayes. "Those guys were supposed to run," he said. "They aren't running. They're hiding behind the trucks."

"Under the trucks, too," Hayes said.

"The plan ain't working," Billy Two agreed.

"Time for a new plan," Hayes said. "If we can't make them run into our cross fire, we're going to have to take our cross fire to them."

"I don't like the sound of that," Nanos said.

Billy Two was already adjusting the extra 30-round magazines he had stuffed under his belt.

"Come on, Alex," Starfoot said. "They don't stand a chance."

"Is that supposed to be a joke?"

Both Hayes and Billy ignored him and prepared to rush headlong into the breach. Nanos couldn't let his friends go to hell alone. "All right, all right," he said, "but I want to lead the charge."

"Lead away," Hayes told him.

The Greek sucked down a deep breath, made sure his weapon was on full-auto and that the safety was off, then hurled himself around the corner.

He could see two trucks. The one on his left faced him, the one on his right was headed the other way. In front of the truck on the left were five Soviets, all armed. Beside the truck on the right were three more.

All eight of them were looking the other way.

The only soldier who saw them come around the corner was standing on the running board of the facing truck, talking to the truck driver in urgent tones. He cut loose with an AK.

The three SOBs scattered, dodging slugs.

Nanos got his H&K up and slashed a 10-round burst across the truck's windshield, busting holes in it from left to right. The guy on the running board took a solid hit to the throat and toppled. The driver's head disappeared as blood misted the inside of the windshield.

Their presence was no longer a secret.

The five in front of the truck turned to bring their weapons to bear. As did the three by the side.

Confidence in the abilities of others is the key to a successful hardstrike. Nanos knew that he could trust Billy and Claude to handle the men by the bumper. Just as they knew he would take out the other three. Alex turned away from the men aiming at him and fired a 20-round burst into the trio. His shots tracked in a near draftsman's line across the row of faces. Gunfire exploded from the truck front, and ComBloc steel whistled past his neck.

Alex glanced over his shoulder.

Hayes and Billy had waded into the five, running right up their noses. Nine millimeter slugs went through and through, stitching vents in the truck radiator. As bodies slumped, blood and antifreeze pooled together on the night street.

The Greek ripped out the spent clip and replaced it, kneeling against a set of double wheels. He peeked around the edge of the tread, under the truck on the right. Orange lights winked at him. Bullets screamed. As he jerked back, the tires blew from multiple hits, dropping the truck onto its rims.

There was an entire advisory committee under there.

Nanos wished to hell he'd had a frag grenade.

More gunfire erupted from under the 6x6.

Then the committee started to abandon the truck. They came out shooting.

Hayes and Billy took the ones coming out from under the side and Nanos took the ones scooting out the rear. After a frenzied minute it was all over. Every one of them was down and out.

"What made them come out from under there like that?" Alex said. "Like they were shot out of a cannon." He quickly reloaded, then checked under the truck.

Two blackened faces beamed at him over their autoweapons.

"Doc! And the Colonel!" he said.

The pair crawled out.

"What did you do under there?" Nanos asked.

"Trade secret," Barrabas told him.

"Come on!"

Barrabas winked at Lee, who said, "I know a good bit of Russian."

"So?"

"So, do you want to know Russian for 'Eeek! It's a mouse!'?"

"Sorry I asked."

"Let's make sure the other side is secure," Barrabas said.

They climbed over the trucks and down to the street. It was a total wipeout on that end, too. Barrabas waved to Jessup and O'Toole, then joined the others in the bed of the money truck.

"God, what a mess!" Lee Hatton said.

"You've heard of 'blood money,' haven't you?" Billy Two asked.

"Hayes," Barrabas said, "see if this thing still runs. If it doesn't we're going to have to offload all these sacks."

Hayes hopped down and squeezed around the side of the truck. He got in the cab and turned the key. It started on the first try.

"At last," Barrabas said. "We finally snag ourselves a break."

Walker Jessup came up, puffing. He leaned his backside against the open tailgate and mopped his face with a handkerchief. After a moment, when he could speak, he said, "We've recovered the money. That's great. What about Heiss?"

"Not here," Barrabas said grimly. "I checked every corpse. He must've run before this trap was sprung."

"I think there's only one place he could be heading. The refugee camp in the north where he and Lalarva were so anxious to shoot their live TV show. If he already had an escape route to Sudan worked out, he'll use it now to get out from under this fiasco with a whole skin."

"It's time to go," Barrabas said. "Billy, get up there in front with Claude. Help him back out of this mess. We'll pick up Liam on the way out."

"We're going to the Swiss embassy?" Jessup said.

Barrabas shook his head. "Eritrea."

"But the money..."

"Heiss isn't going to get away!"

19

Esther Walatta held on to the side of the stake truck as it jittered over a long section of rutted dirt road. She had discovered during the night that standing up in a truck bed was much easier than sitting. The bounces were not so rough.

She had never ridden in a motor vehicle before last evening. After a mere twelve hours of practice, she had become an old hand at the business of being a passenger. It wasn't nearly as hard as it looked.

She would never have taken the ride offered by the strange white men in bright shirts if it hadn't been for her son, Deneke, whom she had lost, then found again. The baby had been so good, so quiet for so long, despite his suffering. She had to get him to food and medicine as soon as possible, even if that meant getting on the back of an open truck.

Esther and Deneke were not alone in the back. There were many heavy boxes of all shapes. There was also another little family of hitchhikers. A woman and two daughters, both in their early teens.

The other woman spoke a few words of Tigre. That coupled with crude sign language had been enough to get it across to Esther that the truck was going to a refugee camp where there would be help.

Esther had tried to sleep during the night but the jumping of the truck was so terrible that she was afraid it would wake her son. She wanted him to sleep, to dream, to stay asleep until there was hope. So, she had stood the whole night with the rag-wrapped bundle in her arms, cradling him to her.

The truck had stopped only once, for the men to relieve themselves. They seemed friendly, smiled often, and though they tried to communicate with her, they were unable to make her understand the reason for their presence in her country or the purpose of the heavy boxes.

In sunlight now, Esther dozed on her feet, swaying against the wooden sides of the truck. She didn't notice that they were turning off the main road, down a side track. The countryside was rolling, sun-blasted, spotted with the occasional acacia. It looked like everywhere she had been for the last two months.

On the side of the road other pilgrims trudged. There was no room for them in the truck. They, too, were headed for salvation.

The other woman pulled at the hem of Esther's shift, waking her. She pointed ahead, smiling.

The camp loomed in the distance. Not as large as the one she had lost Deneke in, it stood in a shallow valley between low hills. She could see the smoke from the cook fires. Esther hugged Deneke to her, making cooing noises in the back of her throat. Her eyes brimmed with tears.

The other woman understood her pain. Her joy. She reached out her hands.

Esther did not understand.

The woman pointed at Deneke, then made a cradle of her arms. She wanted to hold him.

Esther shook her head. She would not let anyone take her baby again.

The woman said something to her daughters, who looked at Esther sympathetically. One of them answered back. The mother nodded.

Esther thought the matter was closed, but evidently it was not.

The other woman made a series of hand gestures at her, giving Esther to understand that she just wanted to see the baby, that she didn't have to hold it.

Esther refused again, afraid that unwrapping the boy might wake him. The other woman would not give up. She held her hands together in the universal attitude of prayer, then repeated her request.

What could Esther do?

The woman had been kind to her.

And one kindness deserved another.

Esther let herself slip down to the floor of the truck bed and sat there cross-legged as she began to undo the wrappings. Rather than unwinding them all, she merely loosened them and then spread them apart, exposing the curve of Deneke's back to the woman and her daughters.

The smiles on their faces suddenly looked dead. The two daughters quickly averted their eyes.

Esther felt a pang of hurt.

Was her son not a handsome child?

The other woman smiled reassuringly and nodded, patting her on the arm. Then she pulled the covering back over Deneke. There were tears in her eyes, now. She sat back and stared at her own dusty bare feet. The other woman knew that Esther, out of sadness or grief, or both, had taken an object and was treating it like a much-adored child.

The other woman could not read English.

If she could have, she would have understood the meaning of the words printed on the baby's back: Front Toward Enemy.

"IT'LL GET ME on the cover of *Time*!" the rock singer exclaimed as he and his personal manager rode to the Addis airport in a hired limo.

"Probably," the man in the black leather suit and matching fedora said.

"And as a direct result my next LP will go instant platinum."

"Undoubtedly."

"The idea is a stroke of pure genius."

"You're right."

"Then why didn't you think of it?"

"Huh?"

Smooth beat his fist against the glass between the passenger and driver compartment. "Stop!" he ordered the driver. Then he opened the door and said, "Out!"

"You can't do this to me!" the manager said. "After all I've done for you..."

Smooth reached into the floppy top of his calf-high suede boots and took out a four-barreled .357 Magnum derringer. "Peaches says 'Get out the car, dirtface.'"

The manager got out.

Smooth slammed the door shut and hit the glass barrier with his fist. The limo surged away, leaving the manager doing a hat dance in the dust. The singer laughed as he put Peaches back in her ankle holster.

He had it all figured.

The way around the Dergue.

They wouldn't give him permission to personally deliver his tons of grain to the needy. An event that was intended to be the stunning, emotional climax of the world-class music video he was filming. But of course they would give permission to the La-larva Crusade '85 to shoot a live satellite fund-raising TV show, pandering to a well-known rip-off artist under federal investigation.

Smooth had no clue what he had done to deserve the Dergue's scorn. He had a highly evolved hairdo. He sang in falsetto. He wore pink boots. All expressions of his personal freedom, his robust individuality. Perhaps that was it, he thought, as the limo pulled into the airport. It was all political. He was making this profound statement, no, an attack, an attack on the very foundation of their stinking failed Marxist state. That's what they couldn't handle.

He was going to show them.

The limo stopped at a freight cargo gate and Smooth got out. He flashed his ID to the army guard at the gate. "Just want to check my plane's cargo," he said, indicating the C-130 parked on the tarmac on the other side of the fence.

As he passed through the gate, he saw his rented pilot and copilot start up the gangway to the flight cabin. He broke into a trot. By the time he reached the bottom of the stairs the crew was inside the plane. Smooth took the stairs three at a time, bursting into the cabin out of breath.

"Good morning, sir," the pilot said.

The copilot repeated the greeting, swiveling in his chair to smile up at the boss.

Smooth said, "Start it up. Let's get out of here."

The pilots exchanged stunned looks.

"We can't do that, sir," the copilot said. "We haven't filed a flight plan. We don't even know where we're going."

"Eritrea," Smooth said.

"Now, wait a minute," the pilot said. "We don't have permission to go there, even if we had filed a flight plan."

"When your people said you wanted us to meet you here there wasn't any mention of a takeoff or a trip into disputed territory," the copilot told him.

"Forget it, Fred," the pilot said, pushing up from his chair. "This guy is nuts. We're leaving. Come on."

"Peaches says no," Smooth said, dipping into his boot top and coming up with the derringer. He pushed it into the pilot's astonished face. "Peaches says get this pile of junk up."

The pilot returned to his seat. "They'll probably shoot us out of the air," he said.

Smooth wasn't even listening. He was thinking about what a big splash he was going to make on live satellite TV.

20

Dr. Lalarva had convinced Heiss to slow down soon after they had left the outskirts of Addis. Going 100-plus around turns banked the wrong way, over roads that had potholes the size of beachballs, was definitely hazardous to the health.

Even though Heiss had backed off on the gas, Lalarva still couldn't relax. He had tried to sleep while they wound their way north, but the idea of sleeping in the company of someone like Heiss was unthinkable.

When they traded off behind the wheel, Heiss didn't seem to have any problem getting to sleep. He actually snored so loudly that Lalarva had been forced to open a window, the rush of air helping to mask the sound of sawing wood. Every hour or so, while he was driving, Lalarva decided that the time was right to kill his business partner, to do it while he slept.

But was Heiss really sleeping?

Or was it a ruse to draw Lalarva out, to make him commit to the deed?

Lalarva could see himself suddenly looking into the muzzle of Heiss's gun, which the man had kept hidden inside his coat or on the seat beside him. He could see Heiss smirking as he pulled the trigger.

Every hour, Lalarva had decided to wait just a little longer. Then it had started to get light and it was too late. He was sure the man was awake now, playing possum.

As he drove over the dirt track, he kicked himself for not swallowing his fear and doing the killing at night. It would have been so much easier in the dark. Easier to put a gun to a sleeping man's head. Easier to avoid looking at the wrecked aftermath.

"How much farther is it?" said the man with his eyes closed.

Lalarva's heart trip-hammered. Heiss was awake. He thanked God he hadn't tried anything, yet.

"I said how much farther is it?" Heiss repeated, an edge of irritation creeping into his voice.

"Uhh, we have another fifteen minutes to go," Lalarva managed. "It would be sooner but for this damned road."

"Are you okay to keep on driving?"

Lalarva realized that this was his big, perhaps his final opportunity. "My neck is bothering me some. If you're awake why don't take over for the last bit."

Heiss rubbed his eyes and yawned. "Sure, pull over anywhere."

Lalarva slowed the car to a crawl, then swung it off the track and onto a rounded shoulder pocked with softball-sized rocks. He turned off the engine. "I'd like to get out and stretch my legs," he said, opening the driver door.

"Yeah, why not?"

Lalarva had no plan. He felt he needed a plan. "I'm going to walk over that way."

"Don't be too long," Heiss said.

The mail-order Ph.D. in sociology grunted assent. He strode off purposefully, then slowed after he was over the top of the low rise. The view was appalling. Everything was dead. Every blade of grass. There were no trees or bushes. All had been stripped away by humans and animals. Lalarva found himself again homesick for his "valley," for its carefully vacuumed Astroturf lawns, its plastic rubber trees in gaily painted Mexican pots. In the valley there could never be a disaster like the one that confronted him. Even if all the rivers dried up, the landscape gardeners passed away, the plastic would remain.

Soon, he would be home, he told himself. But first, he had to deal with Heiss. He absolutely had to.

He thought about keeping the AMT in his pocket, shooting the man through the pocket. That way he would be sure to get the drop on him. But he hadn't practiced shooting through his pocket. He wasn't sure he could hit anything. He would have to take a body shot, either front or back.

Lalarva winced.

The .380 wasn't a big punch cartridge. The guy in the gun store had warned him of that. He'd said, "Go for the head and it'll work fine."

And what would happen if the first shot didn't disable Heiss? The man was a trained killer. Wounded he would be a force Lalarva could not handle.

So, it was back to the head.

But how to get the gun there without blowing the element of surprise?

A distraction.

Even something fleeting.

He would have his hand on the gun and when the moment came he would act. He had to.

Lalarva turned and walked briskly back to the Mercedes. The sooner the deed was behind him, the better.

SMOOTH SAT in the navigator's seat, humming the same two-measure phrase over and over.

Every once in a while either the pilot or the co-pilot would glance back from the controls and give him an irritated look.

"I should've brought along a guitar," Smooth complained. "I've got this great idea for a song. It came to me as we took off. Need a guitar to really flesh it out."

The pilots said nothing.

"I guess I could work on the beat, though," he said, pulling a couple of pencils out of a cup on the navigator's desk. He started whacking the desktop with the pencils as he hummed.

The pilots slipped their headsets on. The captain reached out and twisted up the volume.

Smooth noticed.

He leaned forward, took hold of the pilot's right headset, pulled it away from his ear and pushed Peaches into the void. "Don't you want to help me write a hit song?" he asked.

The pilot removed his headset. So did the copilot.

Smooth resumed his combination humming and pencil tapping, occasionally asking for an "honest opinion."

The opinion he got was always the same: "Great, love it."

The creative process was interrupted by a crackle of radio transmission. To Smooth, it was just a bunch of numbers and letters. It made the flyers sweat bullets.

"Mr. Smooth," the captain said, "that was a challenge from a MiG, six thousand feet above and behind us. He wants to know if we're the C-130 who took off from Addis without clearance.''

''Stonewall him.''

''No, you don't understand. If we don't give him the right answers, he's going to shoot us down.''

Smooth furrowed his brow. ''Tell him we're not that C-130, that we're on a mercy flight.''

''Jesus!'' the copilot said.

The pilot put his hand on his second-in-command's shoulder. ''What you don't know,'' he said to Smooth, in a voice full of forced calm, ''is that the MiG pilot is probably a Yemeni. He hasn't strafed anything bigger than a camel cart for a week. He's sitting up there in his form-fitting chair, with the cannon button under his thumb. He's looking at us in his gunsights and he's in love. In love. Do you follow me?''

Smooth nodded.

''If we give him any bullshit he's got a license to put us tail up in the dirt.''

''How far away are we from the camp?''

The copilot threw up his hands.

''No, wait, let's see,'' the pilot said, checking the chart. ''About five minutes.''

''If we tell him this is a classified military flight, how much time will it buy us?''

''God, not more than five. Two, maybe.''

"Okay, let's do this. We give him a phony flight number, let it ride for two minutes, then send up a Mayday."

"You've got to be kidding!" the copilot said.

"It would be much safer," the pilot said, "to turn this airplane around and fly it back to Addis. I'm sure the government will be understanding, what with your being a foreigner and upset with the bureaucracy."

"Peaches says no."

"Look, rock star," the copilot said, "if we send a Mayday the Yemeni is going to follow us down. If we don't crash this plane as advertised, he's going to crash it for us."

"So we crash it, who cares? I'm insured up to here. The air transport company gets a brand-new plane."

"We can't crash it down there and walk away."

"He's right," the pilot said. "The ground's too rough. We'll nose into the side of a hill and that will be that."

"I've seen pictures of this camp," Smooth said. "There's a nice flat stretch right in front of it."

"How long?" the copilot said.

"What?"

"How long a flat stretch? Do you know what kind of runway a plane like this needs?"

"Peaches says the discussion is over," Smooth said. "Peaches says get on the horn. You know what to tell him."

21

Heiss was behind the wheel, waiting for him, when Lalarva returned. He got into the passenger seat and shut the door.

"Have a nice walk?" Heiss said as he fishtailed the Mercedes in the dirt, bouncing it back onto the road.

Lalarva shrugged. Inside, he was scared. Scared that Heiss knew what he was about to pull, that the intent to murder was somehow written in his eyes. He felt like he had to talk.

"I guess I'm a little nervous about this live satellite thing," he said.

"Why? You've done all kinds of TV."

"Not like this. The shows we usually broadcast are film or videotape. Anything that goes wrong can be edited out before air. This satellite thing, if there's a foul-up, it stands."

Heiss laughed. It was an unpleasant sound.

"TV is an art."

"Stealing from widows and orphans is the art; TV is the blunt instrument," Heiss countered.

Lalarva felt his face flush. He was getting mad. That was good. That would make it easier. And the madder he got, the more Heiss seemed to enjoy it. He was driving with one hand on the wheel. That wasn't so good. When the other hand went back on, Heiss was dead.

"You don't even know what I'm talking about," he told Heiss.

"Oh, I know. You're telling me that you're not a fleabag hypocrite. I don't happen to believe it."

Lalarva watched as the man shifted in his seat. His left hand remained in his lap.

"You want an example?" Heiss asked.

"No, I don't."

"This camp we're going to. It's not really one of yours. It has nothing to do with Crusade '85 except that it's a backdrop for your plea for more money. The refugees who appear on camera are never going to see a dime of anything you collect."

Lalarva said nothing.

"The difference between you and me, Dr. Lalarva, is that I can take the money, dump on the starving people and still like myself the next morning. You have to play games, play TV star, big-shot talent. Hey, you don't even have the talent to rob a grave."

Lalarva's right hand slipped into his coat pocket. His fingers closed around the AMT's grip. He was going to do it. He was going to do it right now.

"Say, is that your soon-to-be-famous refugee camp up there?" Heiss said.

Lalarva froze. It was true. They were on the camp grounds already. Brown people with vacant dolls' eyes sat on the edge of the road, sifting dirt between their fingers, looking for something to eat.

"Do I follow the road right up the hill?" Heiss said.

"Uh, yes. Up the hill."

Lalarva felt like putting the gun to his own head. How many opportunities had he wasted? And now he was going to have to do it in the middle of a crowd!

The TV crew was already set up near the camp's food shack. Lalarva could see the crew members all the way across the compound. They all wore loud sportshirts.

As Heiss made the last turn before entering the actual living area, a plane passed overhead. A very big plane. The roar of its engine was so loud that it shook the car.

"What the hell?" Heiss exclaimed, hitting the brakes and sticking his head out the driver window. "That's a Hercules. It looks like it's going to try and land here."

Lalarva saw the plane bank and come slowly back around.

"It is going to land," Heiss said, jumping out of the car.

Lalarva got out, too.

"It's got an escort, too," Heiss said, his finger following the silver glint of a jet fighter streaking overhead.

"That plane can't land here," Lalarva said.

"You know it, I know it, but don't tell the pilot, because here he comes."

Lalarva tore his gaze from the descending C-130. Every other eye in the camp was riveted to the sky. Heiss was so enthralled that he was holding his breath. If there was a perfect moment to commit a murder, it was now.

He hurried around the back of the car, coming up behind the oblivious Heiss. The Hercules was forty feet above the ground and losing altitude fast. The moment of impact, Lalarva thought as he drew the small autopistol from his pocket, keeping it hidden in the palm of his hand.

When the plane swept by their position on its final run, it was less than ten feet up.

Heiss turned his head to follow its course. "This one's going to go off like the Fourth of July!" he cried.

Lalarva raised the gun, thumbed off the safety, and held the muzzle two inches from the back of Heiss's head.

IT'S GOING TO WORK just fine, you'll see," Smooth told the pilots as they brought the cargo plane down with its landing gear retracted.

"God! Look at that terrain!" the copilot gasped.

"We can't abort, now," the pilot said. "Hang on to your balls!"

In his mind, Smooth visualized the landing. It would be a graceful sweep, like a skater's curve on ice. The huge plane turning slightly as it slowed, turning as if to offer its bulging side to the starving refugees. As soon as the plane stopped, he would leap out the cargo door in his pink boots, his hedgehog hair, spilling tons upon tons of priceless, golden grain behind him.

It was a wonderful, poetic vision.

And he fully intended to use it somehow on his next LP, the one that was to go platinum on advance orders.

Culture's great loss, it was not meant to be.

LALARVA WATCHED THE PLANE and Heiss at the same time. When the fusilage touched ground, he started to squeeze the trigger. A split second before the trigger's break point and the snap of its firing pin, the C-130 exploded.

It was more like Hiroshima than the Fourth of July.

The little pistol's report was utterly lost in the savage detonation, a blast that shattered the huge airplane, sending wings as big as football fields cartwheeling away from a seething ball of fire.

Lalarva was so stunned by the force that for a moment he must have blacked out. He was suddenly aware of the fact that he was sitting on the ground, instead of standing. The AMT was in his outstretched right hand, its slide all the way back, indicating that he had fired all five rounds.

He looked at the automatic in amazement. He couldn't remember pulling the trigger all the way once, let alone five times.

Then he saw Heiss.

His immediate instinct was to shove the gun back in his pocket. His second instinct was to look around and see if anyone in the camp was looking, if anyone had by accident seen the murder.

He had nothing to fear in that regard.

Everyone, refugees, doctors, TV people, were all stunned into immobility by the scale of the disaster. Fire and smoke pillared up from the crash sight, five hundred feet and rising. It drew the human gaze like a magnet.

Lalarva rose shakily to his feet. The Mercedes blocked the camp's view of Heiss. As far as it was concerned, he had never been born.

The body lay still on its face.

Lalarva bent down over it, forcing himself to peer at the back of the head. There was much blood, as one would expect. It streamed sluggishly down the sides of Heiss's neck. Lalarva had to be sure. He put his fingers to the throat of the still-warm body, searching for a pulse.

Blood got on his fingers and he jerked them back, wiping them in the dirt to clean them off.

If there was a pulse, he couldn't find it.

Lalarva stood again, put his hands on his hips and surveyed the camp. What he was looking for turned out to be behind him, away from the people who, though they still stared in awe, had begun to talk to each other, to look around for friends to share the experience with.

He grabbed hold of Heiss's ankles and dragged him away, over the rough ground, to the place where the camp dead were buried. Communally. He took Heiss's papers and valuables and then rolled him up in an Ethiopian shroud, a ragged sheet of muslin. He then dumped the body into the long, shallow pit, stepping in to push aside other corpses so the new one would be closer to the bottom.

Satisfied, Lalarva climbed out of the open grave and ran for the Mercedes. He did not look back.

22

Esther Walatta arrived at the camp too late for the midday meal, but she had arrived in style. The white men with the truck had driven it right up through the middle of camp. All the refugees stopped what they were doing and looked. The woman and her two daughters waved. Esther just looked back, and seeing the fear on some of the people's faces made her feel proud to have conquered her own.

The white men helped her out of the truck and then began unloading the heavy boxes. Some other white men who were already there joined in and soon they had everything piled in one spot.

With mealtime hours away, Esther had nothing to do. To keep her mind off her weakness, she watched the white men work.

From the boxes they pulled incredible things. And they knew what each thing was for.

Esther rocked Deneke and watched from the shade of the corrugated tin roof of the food shack.

Others watched, too, but not knowing the white men as well as she did, they kept a safe distance.

She was half dozing when the plane flew over the first time. The noise it made woke her up. She saw the size of the shadow it cast on the ground, a shadow as big as a mountain, and drew her legs up to her chest. She hugged her baby tight.

One of the white men saw her fear and knelt beside her for a moment. He spoke words she did not understand and smiled. He pointed at the plane and waved it off as if it was the most inconsequential of things. Then he pointed at himself and said, "Randall."

Esther understood that. "Esther," she told him, indicating herself. And then pointed at the bundle of rags and said, "Deneke."

The white man, Randall, was trying to say the name when the plane came around a second time, lower. He looked at it the way Esther had when she first saw it. He seemed to get very excited and so did the other white men.

Esther watched the plane come down and then explode. She didn't understand and it made her afraid and cold inside. Colder than she had ever been. The others stood and watched the fire rise into the sky, but Esther stayed in the shade. She lay on her side on the ground and put Deneke next to her.

She fell into a sleep of deep and perfect peace and after a short time stopped breathing.

DR. TUTTLE LALARVA was one minute to air.

His makeup was right: extra heavy on the bronzer to give him that rugged, outdoor look. His clothes were right: a powder-blue polyester safari suit and matching safari hat with leopard-skin hatband. His attitude was right: even as he watched one of the crewmen count him down to red light his chin and lower lip began to quiver.

Look out world, he thought as the crewman pointed him "on."

Back in the Encino, California, studios of the Lalarva Crusade World Headquarters, someone was turning up the intro music as the camera filled with Dr. Tuttle Lalarva's compassionate face and a backdrop of huddled, malnourished human beings.

"I'm here with friends," he began, gesturing over his shoulder, his eyes never leaving the camera. "I'd like you to know them. To know them as I do."

Back in the San Fernando Valley, someone at the controls played with the incoming video signals, overlaying two images. The stronger was Lalarva's face; the weaker an agonizingly slow panning shot of the camp residents.

"I'm going to bring them into your lives tonight," he said, his voice going suddenly gravely with suppressed emotion, "in the hope that what you see will change you forever. And for the better."

The camera pulled back to show Lalarva down on one knee in the midst of a sea of prostrate people.

"This is my family," he said.

The camera zoomed back farther, making Lalarva half-size in a much bigger sea.

"This is your family," he said.

Another reverse zoom and the man in powder blue is a tiny speck in an enormous human mass.

"This is our family."

The camera returned to the original kneeling shot.

"Many times in the past I have shown you suffering on a terrible scale, pictures like the ones you have just seen. And because of those pictures and the sense of outraged decency that they instilled in your good hearts, you saw fit to contribute to our truly noble cause. Tonight I will be showing you hunger one to one, face-to-face. It will be as if you had looked over your garden fence and there, sitting huddled in the shadow, your own next-door neighbor, the man you bowl with on Thursdays, the lady who loves cats, the teenager who baby-sits: hollow-cheeked, glassy eyed, spindly limbed, dying."

He spread his arms wide, a heavy gold-link chain bracelet dangling from one wrist, a Rolex Daydate on the other. With his open arms he seemed to embrace the half-naked multitudes.

"These are people, too."

He waved an interpreter over and sat down beside a young mother. Through the interpreter, Lalarva and the video audience learned the story of the woman, her personal disaster. Lalarva maintained control of the interview, breaking in on the interpreter's words to ask questions, not only of the refugee, but the viewer at home. He asked them how they liked the show so far. He asked them what they thought of the intimate details of the woman's tragedy; not because he expected an answer, but because he wanted to retell the story, himself, to wrap his dulcet tones around the words, to make it his story.

When he felt he had gotten all the mileage he could out of the case history, he moved on, working his way through the crowd. Occasionally, as the interpreter relayed something particularly gutwrenching, the camera would stray from the face of the victim, and the screen would fill with Lalarva's face, reacting. Chin and lower lip quivering, eyes brimming with tears behind the purple-tinted lenses. As he was moved, so was his audience. He was their intercessor, he suffered the torments of hell so that they could get off the easy way, by digging in their pockets, writing checks.

As the show unfolded, Lalarva could feel the blossoming of his mastery over the medium, his innate ability to recognize and seize the video moment, that transitory perfect melding of image, sound and emotion.

When, during a station break, one of his crew ran up and told him that a young woman with a baby had just died, Lalarva seized the opportunity to encapsulate his message in the tale of a new orphan. For that he needed a clear set and tight focus.

"Get these others out!" he shouted, waving his arms, stamping his feet. "And bring the baby to me!"

The refugees were easily frightened. They fled to the edges of the camp, leaving Dr. Lalarva alone on a bleak stage. For more than a hundred yards in all directions there was only brown dust. In the dust were thousands upon thousands of mingled footprints.

The crewman rushed from the food shack carrying a rag-wrapped bundle in his arms.

"And cue!" Lalarva was told.

He looked into the camera and said nothing for five beats, letting his brimming eyes and trembling lip do the talking. When he did speak, his voice cracked and squeaked.

"A friend of mine just lost his mother," he said, pushing thumb and forefinger up under his glasses to pinch the bridge of his nose, letting the camera see the tears breaking free of his tightly shut eyes and rolling down his cheeks. "A dear little friend of mine."

Lalarva held out his arms to receive the bundle.

It was still thirty feet away.

The break in timing would have destroyed the moment for a lesser personage. Lalarva milked it, throwing down his arms, beaming through the tears. "Here he comes, here he comes now," he said.

The crewman passed him the tiny bundle.

"How tiny you are," Lalarva said, holding the muslin cocoon in one hand. He looked past the cocoon, straight into the hearts of twenty million people and said, "How tiny you are, Danny K., to have lost your mother."

The power of the moment was a tangible thing.

He let it go, let it fade like the final note of a symphony. But he wasn't done with little Danny K., yet.

"Let's see your pretty face, child," Lalarva said, cradling the bundle in the crook of his arm as he peeled aside the windings.

When he saw that the thing in the wrapping was not a baby, but some metallic object, he knew the show was blown. There was no way to recover from such a fiasco. His face sagged and the tears that flowed down his face were genuine, a TV first. His fingers trembled as they toyed aimlessly with the winding. The wrappings came away and his eyes widened in horror.

Front Toward Enemy

He did not mean to drop it.

Dropping it was the last thing in the world he wanted to do. But if he had just dropped it, had let it fall to the dirt, nothing would have happened, except that the fraud of his "dear little friend" would have been unveiled to a global audience. The armed Claymore would not have exploded.

Drop it, he did.

As it slipped from his grasp he tried desperately to keep it from hitting the ground. The rag and wire were still draped over and between his fingers. To bring the falling mine back to him, he pulled. The mine came back to him, but not in the way he had anticipated.

The encased kilo of composition C-4 detonated with a blistering whack, sending thousands of steel ball bearings into flight. The impact blew Dr. Tuttle Lalarva apart. Blood mist, dust and plastic explosive smoke hung over the spot where he had stood. But he was not entirely gone.

When Lalarva leapt from the camera's frame, the cameraman, a former network baseball veteran, instinctively tilted his lens up, following the much-perforated mail-order Ph.D.'s seventy-five foot arc in the air.

Twenty million pairs of eyes saw an unrecognizable hulk rising, cartwheeling, spraying red, then falling to earth. It bounced once on landing.

"Sweet Jesus!" the crewman named Randall gasped, throwing himself to the ground. The air was filled with singing death. Ball bearings slammed the food shack, pelted the crew trucks. And then it was over

For a good two minutes, the camera remained locked on the thing in the dust.

Then Randall rushed in front of the lens, waving his hands at the operator and an astonished global audience. "That's all!" he cried. "Turn it off, Louie! For God's sake, Louie, turn it off!"

23

Barrabas double-clutched and downshifted, holding the 6x6 tight to the inside of the turn, a hairbreadth from the jutting rock outcrop it bent around. The outside of the turn was lost to view, buried in fine, wind-drifted dust, dust like brown talcum powder. He had good reason to be careful. They'd had to dig out twice already. It had cost them precious time.

The all-night ride from Addis had been hairy. At five checkpoints they'd had to produce the Crusade '85 travel documents and, with SMG muzzles poking in their faces, wait patiently for permission to pass on. After daybreak they had crossed over into no-man's land and the tension had gotten even worse. The guerrillas loved to ambush aid trucks for food; bored government MiG pilots strafed them for fun.

Barrabas powered up the slight incline and when the dirt road flattened out, double-clutched again and slipped into a higher gear.

Nothing disastrous had happened, yet. The only close call was humorous in retrospect. When Jessup was driving, a wild camel, spooked by the engine noise, had darted out into the road in front of them. Instead of ducking back into the bush, the panicked creature continued to flee ahead of them. The fat man had had to slam on the brakes to keep from hitting it.

As they rounded another bend, Dr. Lee, who sat beside Barrabas in the passenger seat, pointed at a plume of oily black smoke rising high into the sky. "Look at that!" she said. "What the hell is it?"

It was only a few miles away.

"Could be a downed plane," he said.

"And close to the refugee camp," Lee added.

"We'll find out soon enough."

After a long silence the woman doctor said, "Maybe it's Heiss."

Barrabas grimaced. He wanted Karl Heiss dead, but he didn't want him dead yet. He wanted to be the one to kick out the man's plug; he wanted to watch the light wink out behind those cesspool eyes. His burning desire notwithstanding, the white-haired man had to admit that Heiss being killed by some other hand was preferable to Heiss getting away clean, again. As long as Barrabas could be absolutely sure the man was dead. Too many times in the past he had viewed bullet-riddled or burned bodies believed to be Karl Heiss. And every time it had turned out to be a hoax; every time the man had resurfaced to do more evil.

When the camp finally came into view, it was obvious that the smoke was from a plane crash, though no wreckage was visible. On the other side of the camp Barrabas could see the deep gouge the skidding aircraft had carved in the earth. It had been no mere MiG, either. The wingspan had been tremendous. The center of the fire and smoke was what had once been a small hilltop; now it was a burning crater ringed by a quarter mile of charred ground. The camp's refugee population was not looking at the crash site. They were tightly circled around the TV crew in the middle of the compound.

"Over there," Lee said, pointing to their left.

"I see it," Barrabas said. It was a Mercedes four-door sedan. The driver's side had a ragged line of bullet holes stitched across it and the side windows had been completely shot out.

"It's the same one?"

"The same."

He parked the truck by the food shack and then he and the others got out and made their way through the crowd of brown human skeletons. In the middle of the throng the all-white TV crew was gathered around a clear plastic tarp spread on the ground.

One of the crew looked up and saw Barrabas.

"What happened here?" the white-haired man demanded.

The crew members, eager to relate the tale to someone who could understand, all started speaking at once.

"No, wait a minute," Barrabas said, holding up his hands for silence. He pointed at the man who had first seen him. "What's your name?"

"Randall."

"You tell it, Randall. The rest of you keep quiet until he's done."

"Well, first, this big cargo plane tried to land over there," the crewman said. "It was crazy. No way could it land safely. It exploded like a bomb."

"The plane wasn't expected, then?"

"Not by any of us. We thought it might have run out of fuel, but its engines were going as it came in. And it was jet gas that blew up. You can still smell it when the wind shifts."

Barrabas looked down at the plastic tarp at his feet. Under the opaque sheet there was a pile of gristle, gore and bone mixed with shreds of light blue polyester. To know what the tangled heap represented, you had to have seen it before. "Who was he?" Barrabas asked.

"It was Dr. Lalarva," Randall said. "We still can't figure out what happened. He was live on satellite, holding a baby and he dropped it and then everything just blew up."

"Was anyone else hurt?" Lee Hatton asked.

The crewman shook his head. "It was just luck, though. Metal was flying all over the place."

Billy Two bent down and picked something up from the dirt. He rolled it on his palm, then held it up for Barrabas and the others to see. It was a steel ball bearing. "Some baby, Colonel," he said.

"A friggin' Claymore!" Liam O'Toole exclaimed.

Jessup lifted the edge of the tarp. Under it was a pair of glasses, its purple-tinted lenses both fractured. "It was Lalarva, all right," the fat man said.

"I told you he was on TV when it happened," Randall repeated testily. "Hell, we've got it all on tape if you want to see for yourself."

"Maybe later," Barrabas told him. "When Lalarva got here was he with another man?"

Randall shook his head. "No, he was alone." The look the white-haired man gave him made Randall's throat go dry.

"There was no one with him?"

Randall wanted to please the stranger at that moment. He wanted it more than anything. But those heavy-lidded eyes told him, "Don't lie."

"He got here just as the plane crashed. None of us actually saw him pull in."

The other crew members nodded agreement.

"We were all looking at the plane, the fire," Randall continued. "Things were very confused.

He walked up from behind and joined us. I remember looking back at the Mercedes, there was no one in it.''

Barrabas turned away without a word. He pushed his way back through the crowd and walked over to the car. He got in and did a quick but thorough search of glovebox, door pockets, seats and found no clues, nothing whatsoever he could use. He sat back in the driver's seat and stared out the dusty windshield. Daylight was fading, the sky turning quickly from azure to lavender. On the horizon before him, the evening star shone steady and strong. A slight breeze had sprung up. It whispered through the glassless window at his elbow. With the sun down, the air temperature plummeted.

Heiss was gone.

Again.

He had vanished into the chaos between Addis and this squalid camp. For all Barrabas knew he had never even left the capital. For all Barrabas knew he was just over the next rise. Heiss had always had an uncanny instinct for choosing the right time to abandon ship. And when Heiss did duck out, he made sure he left no clear trail for pursuit, only infinite, maddening possibilities.

This time, Nile Barrabas wasn't mad. No outrage, no white-hot fury boiled his blood. At his very core Barrabas was cold. He knew for Heiss and himself, there would be another time, another place.

A faint sound came to him riding on the wind. A jackal caught in a foottrap, perhaps? Or maybe it was the wind, itself, shrieking as it swept over the desolate hills? Whatever it was, it made the hairs stand up on the back of his neck.

And he damned it to hell.

KARL HEISS AWOKE in pitch darkness, a terrible weight pressing the entire front of his body. There was something covering face, touching his chin. The air was musty and dry. He tried to move his arms and he could not. They were pressed tightly to his sides. He felt with his fingers. He was wrapped in cloth. He struggled futilely against his confinement, blind suffocating panic engulfing him, his heart thudding, his head reeling.

Only through a monumental effort of will did he gain control of his fear.

Think, he told himself.

Where are you?

What had happened?

His head ached horribly and he felt sick.

Think!

The last thing he remembered was the plane. He had been watching it come down, anticipating the lovely crash. And then when it had crashed everything had suddenly gone black.

Had he been hit by some of the flying debris?

No, he was too far away and it had happened too fast.

Wait. Lalarva had been standing behind him. Lalarva. Heiss remembered the instant before blackness, a searing heat from behind. The chickenshit bastard had shot him in the back! And bungled it.

Heiss breathed and coughed rackingly. The air was thick with dust. He twisted his shoulders and something on top of him shifted. It felt like a person, only stiff, all hard edges.

Then he knew the truth.

Karl Heiss threw back his head and screamed up into the darkness, through the heaped layers of the dead.

BEHIND NANOS the pressing crowd seemed to melt away. He turned and saw the refugees rushing en masse for the 6x6, a human stampede. "Holy shit, Billy!" he said to the Indian standing beside him. "What is going on?"

The refugees swarmed over the aid truck like ants. They started throwing out the large grain sacks. They were crying with joy.

"They think it's food," Billy Two said.

Neither of them moved.

They watched the starving people rip open bag after bag, spilling the green rectangles of paper onto the ground, rummaging frantically through them, searching in vain for a single grain of rice. Thirty million dollars lay strewn like confetti over the dust. The people were crying again, but not from joy.

Then one of the refugees gathered up an armfull of the paper and walked away from the truck. Others began to do the same thing. Scooping up hundred dollar bills and going their own way.

None of the SOBs made a move to stop them. They watched, spellbound as little fires began to spring up everywhere inside the compound. Little fires surrounded by huddled, half-naked people.

Flames danced modestly from the tiny blazes.

Money burned to beat back the desert's deadly night chill.

Billy Two looked into the face of his old friend, lit by those flickering fires. He reached his hand up, extending a gentle finger and lifted a tear from the Greek's suntanned cheek.

"What's this?" Starfoot said, holding the droplet to the light.

Nanos stared back. A smile played over his mouth and then it was gone. "Same as those," he said, nodding at the tears brimming in the Indian's obsidian eyes.

"It's from the smoke," Billy Two said.

"Yeah," Nanos said. "From the smoke."

Update on Jack Hild

Dear Gold Eagle Books,

I am interested very much in contacting the attorney of the deceased Mr. Jack Hild. I believe Mr. Hild mentioned me and my staff in his will—at least he told us this when he was last in Manila. I am the proprietor of the Happy Time Date Club for beautiful females of good family eager to meet well-to-do male friends. Mr. Hild said that upon his death he was going to provide the money to pay for a new sixty-foot trailer addition to our place of business, to be called the "Hild Memorial Wing."

Your help in this matter would be deeply appreciated.

Sincerely,

Mrs. Cara Marquez-Espinosa

Dear Mrs. Marquez-Espinosa,

Thank you for your recent letter concerning Jack Hild. To the best of our knowledge Mr. Hild is not dead. Oddly enough, you are not the first person to indicate that Jack was going to fund a "memorial wing" of the kind you describe. I doubt that you will be the last.

Kindest regards,

The Editors, Gold Eagle Books

Nile Barrabas and the Soldiers of Barrabas are the

SOBs

by Jack Hild

Nile Barrabas is a nervy son of a bitch who was the last American soldier out of Vietnam and the first man into a new kind of action. His warriors, called the Soldiers of Barrabas, have one very simple ambition: to do what the Marines can't or won't do. Join the Barrabas blitz! Each book hits new heights—this is brawling at its best!

"Nile Barrabas is one tough SOB himself.... A wealth of detail.... SOBs does the job!"
—*West Coast Review of Books*

#1 The Barrabas Run	#6 Red Hammer Down
#2 The Plains of Fire	#7 River of Flesh
#3 Butchers of Eden	#8 Eye of the Fire
#4 Show No Mercy	#9 Some Choose Hell
#5 Gulag War	#10 Vultures of the Horn

GOLD EAGLE

Available wherever paperbacks are sold.

DON PENDLETON'S EXECUTIONER
MACK BOLAN

Sergeant Mercy in Nam . . . The Executioner in the Mafia Wars . . . Colonel John Phoenix in the Terrorist Wars . . . Now Mack Bolan fights his loneliest war! You've never read writing like this before. By fire and maneuver, Bolan will rack up hell in a world shock-tilted by terror. He wages unsanctioned war—everywhere!

GOLD EAGLE

Available wherever paperbacks are sold.

Mack Bolan's

ABLE TEAM

by Dick Stivers

Action writhes in the reader's own street as Able Team's
Carl "Mr. Ironman" Lyons, Pol Blancanales and
Gadgets Schwarz make triple trouble in blazing war. To
these superspecialists, justice is as sharp as a knife. Join
the guys who began it all—Dick Stivers's Able Team!

"This guy has a fertile mind and a great eye for detail.
Dick Stivers is brilliant!"

—Don Pendleton

Able Team titles are available
wherever paperbacks are sold.

GOLD
EAGLE

Mack Bolan's

PHOENIX FORCE

by Gar Wilson

Schooled in guerrilla warfare, equipped with all the latest lethal hardware, Phoenix Force battles the powers of darkness in an endless crusade for freedom, justice and the rights of the individual. Follow the adventures of one of the legends of the genre. Phoenix Force is the free world's foreign legion!

"Gar Wilson is excellent! Raw action attacks the reader on every page."

—*Don Pendleton*

Phoenix Force titles are available wherever paperbacks are sold.

GOLD EAGLE

Take
4 explosive books
plus a
mystery bonus
FREE

Mail to **Gold Eagle Reader Service**

In the U.S.
2504 West Southern Ave.
Tempe, AZ 85282

In Canada
P.O. Box 2800, Station A
5170 Yonge St.,
Willowdale, Ont. M2N 6J3

YEAH! Rush me 4 free Gold Eagle novels and my free mystery bonus. Then send me 6 brand-new novels every other month as they come off the presses. Bill me at the low price of $2.25 each— a 10% saving off the retail price. There are no shipping, handling or other hidden costs. There is no minimum number of books I must buy. I can always return a shipment and cancel at any time. Even if I never buy another book from Gold Eagle, the 4 free novels and the mystery bonus are mine to keep forever.

Name _____ (PLEASE PRINT)

Address _____ Apt. No. _____

City _____ State/Prov. _____ Zip/Postal Code _____

Signature (If under 18, parent or guardian must sign)

This offer is limited to one order per household and not valid to present subscribers. Price is subject to change.

166-BPM-BPGE   4E-SUB-1